A BOY MADE OF SUNSHINE

COLETTE DAVISON

A Boy Made Of Sunshine

ISBN: 9798654152701
Imprint: Independently published

Cover Design: Colette Davison
Edited by: Sarah Chorn
Proofread by: Tanja Ongkiehong

A BOY MADE OF SUNSHINE

A strict older man. A sassy film star. Can opposites attract?

After taking early retirement from the police force, Liam is happy avoiding people and tending to his roses. Or he was, until Felix moves in next door.

Felix is taking a break from his acting career, even though he's on the cusp of stardom. With his cheeky, persistent, and very naughty behaviour, he gets under Liam's skin instantly.

Felix needs someone who can set him boundaries— a man who can handle him firmly, but with love. Liam doesn't think he needs anyone, until Felix brings much needed sunshine into his life.

Will Felix choose stability and love, or a life of glitz and glamour?

A Boy Made of Sunshine is a light hearted gay romance with a grumpy ex-detective, a brash new neighbour, a cute Dalmatian puppy, and lots of brattish behaviour.

PRAISE FOR A BOY MADE OF SUNSHINE

A Boy Made of Sunshine is an unapologetically joyful and completely immersive love story that reminded me why I love MM romance. During the first half of the book, I felt I was being edged by Davison as masterfully as Felix is edged by his Daddy. It was an emotional roller coaster with absolutely no angst and plenty of heart.

This hot AF Daddy kink fluff bomb is one of my favorite reads of 2020.

— AMY BELLOWS

To everyone who made me smile when the world was turned upside down.

1

___

LIAM

There were several reasons why Liam loved his semi-detached house: the south-facing garden was drenched in sunlight for several hours a day, making it perfect for growing his roses; it was almost within sight of the sea; the two houses were alone on their stretch of peaceful country road, and he had a lovely, quiet neighbour, who kept herself to herself. At least he had until she'd passed a few months earlier. A woman, whom Liam presumed to be her daughter, had come with removal men a few days later to clear the house out, and then a For Sale sign had gone up.

It was the middle of spring when the Sale sign was replaced with a Sold sign. It wasn't a bad thing in and of itself. The house wasn't really big enough for a rowdy family, and he knew it was likely to have attracted more mature occupants, perhaps a nice, quiet retired couple.

When a removal van finally arrived in the first week of summer, Liam's hopes that his quiet existence would continue undisturbed were dashed.

He'd never regarded himself as a curtain twitcher before, but he found himself peering out of his bedroom window as three burly men unloaded the large van. The furniture didn't scream 'quiet retired couple' to him. It was too modern, too loud. Who on earth owned a bright purple sofa, for crying out loud? The bed was even worse. It was a huge monstrosity, easily king-sized, and Liam couldn't help but feel sorry for the men carrying it into the house. The bed frame was black, probably made of leather, judging by the way the sunlight made the fabric shine, with a massive surround, part of which looked like some kind of lounge chair. Did it even have a built-in speaker? Who needed a built-in speaker in their *bed*?

His jaw dropped a little more at every item of furniture that was brought into the house. The coffee table looked like it doubled as an aquarium, although thankfully there were no fish in it. There was a bookcase in the shape of a dog, a dining table with what looked like a solid marble top, overstuffed dining chairs, a pool table, and even a bar!

The painting was the last straw.

The canvas and frame combined must have been six feet tall, making the man that had been painted upon it almost life size. Not only was he nude, but he was grasping his cock, his head tilted back slightly, eyes closed, making it obvious that he was in the midst of pleasuring himself. Liam had never been so glad to have no other neighbours. The painting was glorious—he had to adjust himself to make his aching cock more comfortable in his pants—but why in God's name hadn't it been covered up? Clearly, his new neighbour had no decorum whatsoever.

By breathing slowly and deeply, Liam managed to get rid of his partial hard-on by the time the removal men were closing the back of the van up. Almost as if on cue, a flashy sports car arrived, the driver tooting the horn as he pulled up behind the van, right in front of Liam's front gate. Liam held his breath, watching as a young man with mid-brown hair stepped out. He was wearing a black leather jacket, even though it was far too hot for a coat, and had a huge grin plastered on his face. He put his hands on his slender hips and stared at the house for a few moments before inhaling deeply, his chest puffing out as he did so.

Through the window, Liam heard the young man thank the drivers and watched with bulging eyes as he handed them a ridiculous wad of cash. Instantly, Liam wondered if a drug dealer had moved in next door to him. That was all he needed.

Just then, the young man looked directly up at him. His smile widened.

"Hi, neighbour!" he called in an overly cheerful tone, waving his hand high above his head as he spoke. His voice wasn't unpleasant. If anything, it was smoky with a sing-song quality to it.

Liam scowled deeply in return, angry at himself for having been caught snooping. Clearly, he'd got sloppy since his days on the force. He forced himself to wave politely.

As if things couldn't get any worse, the young man opened the car door again and whistled. A Dalmatian puppy with feet that were at least six times too big for it bounded out. Its red collar sparkled in the sunlight against its black-and-white fur. Dear God, was it studded with diamantés? Liam shook his head. His new neighbour had a dog. Dogs barked and howled at all hours of the day and night and dug holes. He didn't want a dog for a neighbour.

The young man knelt down and showered the puppy with strokes and kisses. He *let* the puppy lick his face, making Liam grimace. He knew he should move away from the window, but ended up staying where he was, arms folded across his broad chest as he looked on in disgust. He put all the clues together: ostentatious, mismatched furniture, flashy sports car, leather jacket, expensive dog. Either his new neighbour really was a drug dealer, or he was a playboy. Either way, he obviously had too much money and not enough sense.

His neighbour scooped the puppy up into his arms and then headed right to Liam's gate and into his garden. Liam watched, horrified, as the man walked down his path with easy strides. He glanced up at Liam, grinning as widely as ever, before knocking on the door. Liam didn't move. He didn't want to talk to the fancy playboy with the purple sofa and king-sized bed. He didn't want to exchange platitudes or 'get to know' him. He wanted a quiet, 'keep to themselves' neighbour. He sighed. What he wanted, and what cruel fate had given him, were poles apart. He looked up at his ceiling.

"Why?" he demanded of whatever higher power

there was; not that he really believed there was one. "What have I done to deserve this?"

When the young man knocked again, Liam trudged down the stairs, his feet landing heavily. He practically threw the front door open and scowled down at his neighbour, who was both shorter than him and standing on a lower level, as there was a step to get into the house. The fucking puppy stared at him with the most adorably large brown eyes, making Liam grind his teeth against the cuteness.

"Hi," his neighbour said in that cheerful, sing-song voice. "I'm Felix Lee." He said it in a manner that suggested Liam should know who he was.

God! The guy was so full of himself.

Liam rolled his eyes so hard they almost did a full three-sixty. "You're named after a cat."

Felix laughed loudly and wagged a finger at Liam. His laughter was light and bubbly like champagne. "You're a funny guy. You realise I've heard that one about a thousand times?" He held his hand out. "So I'm named after a cat." He jostled the puppy in his arms. "This is Domino, and you're…?" He arched an eyebrow, clearly waiting for Liam to offer up his name.

Liam tried and failed to place Felix's accent. There was no mistaking that it was English, possibly southern, but there was an American lilt to it, an undercurrent that led Liam to believe Felix spent far too much time watching US sitcoms. On his purple sofa. Or lounging in his ridiculous bed, with the sound blaring out of the speakers.

"Liam Gladstone." Liam grudgingly shook Felix's hand out of politeness.

The young man's grip was firm, his hands smooth as though he'd never done any kind of manual work in his life. That added more credence to the notion that he was a playboy, although Liam couldn't figure out why someone like that would want to move to a sleepy little village near the sea.

"You're not going to have wild parties, are you?" he asked. "Our houses are joined, you know."

Felix chuckled. "I can see that."

"Well?" Liam demanded. He'd spent enough years living in central London, with music from neighbours and passing cars blaring all through the night; he didn't need that kind of noise pollution now that he was retired.

"I'll keep the sound down if I do," Felix said in a carefree tone.

"Do you smoke?" Liam asked. "If you do, I'd rather you didn't smoke in the back garden."

"I don't smoke."

"Drugs?"

Felix smirked. "You know, this is starting to sound like an interrogation, *or* you're asking me to fill in my dating profile. So no, I don't smoke or do drugs. I do enjoy a drink." His forest-green eyes sparkled mischievously. "I'm most definitely single, and you've probably already guessed from my choice in artwork that I'm gay." He scratched Domino's head. "Anything else?"

Liam gaped at him. "I didn't need to know all that," he said gruffly. "It's just..." He inhaled to regain his composure. "This is—*was*—a quiet place to live. I'd like it to stay that way."

"Noted. Hey, do I get to ask you twenty-one questions now?"

"No," Liam snapped.

Felix shrugged. "Shame. I think I'd like to get to know you better, Liam Gladstone. Find out if you're always this grumpy, or if it's just a special occasion."

"I'm not—!" Liam began, but then shut his mouth.

He'd been goaded enough times while he'd been on the police force to know not to rise to it. There was no reason for this brash, insolent young man to get under his skin, but he was anyway.

"Was there anything else?" he demanded.

Felix stared at him thoughtfully for several moments, smiling in amusement. "Not right now. I'll let you know if I think of anything, though. It was nice meeting you, Liam Gladstone."

"Stop calling me that," Liam snarled.

"It's your name, isn't it?"

"Yes, but..." Liam sighed and pinched the bridge of his nose. "Goodbye."

Felix waggled his fingers in a wave. "Bye, Liam Gladstone."

Liam would have slammed the door in his face, except Felix turned on his heel and set off down the path before he had a chance. He shut the door with less force than he wanted, turned, and leant against it, puffing out a breath. He wondered how quickly he could move if he called the estate agent that day. He gritted his teeth. No, he wasn't going to be driven out of his house by an annoying neighbour. He would simply ignore Felix and the puppy as if they didn't even exist. Simple.

2

FELIX

Felix put Domino down on the dated hallway carpet and then took in the house. *His* house. It might not have been a place he'd have picked for himself, but Emma, his agent, had followed his brief to a tee: somewhere quiet and pretty, not too big, *not* a party house. It did feel like he should be putting on a pair of slippers and a flat cap and drawing his pension, but redecorating the walls and updating the carpet would go a long way toward making the house feel fresher. Granted, he should probably have arranged all that *before* moving in, but c'est la vie.

He watched as Domino sniffed around and eventually decided to squat and pee.

"Guess I should have taken you outside before exploring the house," Felix said with a shrug. "Come on, little guy."

He patted his thigh, and the puppy raced towards him. They had been working on toilet training while they'd been crashing at Rick's house, but it was definitely an ongoing process. The puppy followed him into the kitchen, where Felix rummaged through boxes until he found pet carpet spray and a cloth. After cleaning the carpet as well as he could with elbow grease, he returned to the kitchen to go outside, Domino following him like a clumsy black-and-white shadow. He had to pause and figure out which of the keys he'd been given would unlock the back door. In his rush to get out, the puppy practically fell out of the house. He recovered quickly and then bounded around the garden, pausing to sniff and pee every few seconds. There was a heady, sweet scent in the air, which Felix couldn't place. He pursed his lips as he stared at the neatly mowed lawn and trimmed hedges and then turned his head towards Liam Gladstone's house, smiling.

"Huh. Guess you're not so grumpy after all," he murmured.

He made a mental note to take something round to thank his neighbour for keeping on top of the garden for him. Well, not for him exactly, but for the future owner of the house. He wondered what he'd need to keep the garden up himself. He'd never been into gardening, nor had his parents, mostly because they'd never had much more than a strip of lawn for kicking a ball about. A lawnmower would be a good start, so that was added to his list of things he'd need to buy. Thinking about it, he probably needed to start writing all this stuff down so he didn't forget something crucial.

While Domino continued to explore the garden, Felix sat down on the back step and soaked up the sunshine. He pulled his phone out of his back pocket and sent Emma a quick text.

—*Moved in okay. Thanks for everything. I'll be in touch when I'm ready to look at scripts again.*

She texted straight back.

—*Speak soon.*

Felix half smiled. Short and to the point, as always.

He stood and called Domino to him so they could go back into the house. He dug Domino's food and bowls out of a box and then left the puppy eating in the kitchen, while he went to check out the rest of the house. The removal men had done a good job of placing his eclectic collection of furniture in relevant rooms. None of it looked at home in the quaintly decorated house, but he didn't mind; it wasn't like any of his furniture went together anyway. He'd just seen cool stuff and bought it, a bit like a wide-eyed kid in a candy shop.

The biggest of the two bedrooms was at the front of the house, overlooking the road, so that was where his bed and the glorious nude painting had been placed. He chuckled as he admired it. The removal men had told him that Liam had been watching them move stuff in, so he'd known that the handsome man had caught an eyeful. Okay, so maybe scandalising his new neighbour on day one hadn't made the best first impression, but there was nothing he could do about it now. Had Liam liked the painting? Maybe one day Felix would find out.

From his bedroom window, he could just about see the sea. It was a flat band of grey between the land and the bright blue sky. Another thing to add to his rapidly growing list of things to do was to find out whether he was allowed to walk Domino on the beach. Hopefully, Liam would know random bits of local information like that.

He wandered through to the back of the house to the only completely empty room. It overlooked the garden and also allowed him to take stock of Liam's garden. How many roses did one guy need? There were dozens of neatly planted roses, in a vast range of colours from Valentine's Day red, through every shade of pink imaginable, to peach, coral, and muted orange. Felix didn't think he'd ever seen so many roses in one place, not even in a florist's shop. What lawn Liam had was neatly cut and trimmed. There was a greenhouse too, though the sun glinting off the glass panes made it impossible for Felix to see inside. He opened the sash window and inhaled the same sweet scent he'd picked up on earlier, except now he knew it emanated from Liam's roses.

He smiled as Liam came into view, moving slowly from rose bush to rose bush, clearly inspecting each one. Felix leant against the wall, arms loosely folded, as he gazed at the mountain of a man. The grey tank top he was wearing showed off his huge muscles, which Felix suspected lots of people were intimidate by. Not him. All *he* could think about was whether, if he wrapped both hands around Liam's biceps, his fingertips would meet. Probably not. He bit his lower lip, unable to smother his smile; not that he tried hard. He wasn't normally into guys with beards, but Liam looked good with one. It was long, reaching to his chest, but was neatly trimmed and shaped. If the man's beard and garden were anything to go by, everything about him was likely to be neat and ordered, nothing like the haphazard chaos of Felix's life.

Like him, Liam had dark brown hair, but it also had lots of coppery highlights which were picked out beautifully by the sun. Felix sighed. Liam was one gorgeously grumpy guy. He'd need to come up with an excuse to pop round and talk to his neighbour again very soon.

Right now, he had to start unpacking. Or maybe not. It would probably be easier to move things for decorators if everything was still in boxes, as long as he could cope with living like that for the next few weeks.

He investigated the bathroom next, wrinkling his nose at the dated blue bathroom suite. It was ugly, but at least the wall tiles were plain white to offset the hideousness. The bathroom was definitely going to have to get ripped out and replaced. A whirlpool bath would be a nice addition, or maybe he could have a patio laid in the garden and buy a jacuzzi. He could imagine lazy evenings spent skinny-dipping in the hot bubbly water, further shocking his massive, handsome neighbour.

He went back downstairs to the kitchen and gave Domino some fuss. It was another room that needed completely gutting. The kitchen units didn't look like they'd been changed since the seventies, but it was clean and serviceable, so could probably be kicked down to the bottom of his priority list; it wasn't like he was any good at cooking.

He sat on the floor with Domino, sighing happily as the puppy licked his fingers. It was weird and exciting to have his own house and perhaps a little overwhelming.

He'd have lots of decisions to make over the coming days, weeks, and months, but he was looking forward to making each and every one of them.

"It's too hot to sit inside," he declared.

Domino stared up at him, big eyes probably agreeing with him.

Felix laughed and opened the kitchen door again, chuckling as the puppy fell over its own feet in its hurry to dash outside. In his excitement, Domino yapped, the high-pitched sound filling the air. From the other side of the fence, Felix heard a gruff grumble. Liam was still outside.

There was an old wooden bench against the six-foot fence that separated their gardens. Felix stepped onto it so he could lean on top of the fence. Liam was in the process of taking a cutting from one of the rose bushes.

"Hi, Liam Gladstone."

Liam's head snapped around to glare at him.

"I just wanted to say thanks for keeping my lawn under control," Felix went on because talking meant he wasn't outright laughing at Liam's surly expression. He'd never before imagined that grumpy could be attractive, but Liam somehow managed it. "At least, I'm guessing it was you."

"It was."

Felix tilted his head. "Do you have a key to the house?" Not that he minded if Liam did, but it would be good to know.

Liam shook his head and pointed to the end of Felix's garden. "There's a back gate."

Felix smacked his forehead lightly. "So there is.

Sometimes I can't see for looking." He raked his teeth over his lower lip. "Your roses are beautiful."

Liam grunted as he transferred the cutting to a small pot.

"Would you mind if I came round and took a closer look at them sometime?"

"Yes," Liam said bluntly.

Not about to be put off by the rebuttal, Felix changed tack. "I need to get some decorating done. Could you recommend anyone?"

"No."

"How long have you lived here?"

Liam hunched his strong, sloping shoulders and turned away, trudging back to the house. He looked like a grumpy bear, Felix decided, bad-tempered, but in a cute, fluffy way.

Just before he went inside, Liam stopped and looked back at Felix. "Will your parents be joining you?"

"Ouch!" Felix said in a light-hearted tone. "I'm not *that* young." He only just resisted calling Liam 'grandpa' by biting his tongue. "I'm twenty-five. I've lived on my own for a few years now, but this is the first time I've bought a house." He knew he was rambling; not that it was necessarily a bad thing. Generally, when his tongue ran off like that, it was a sure sign he was ruffled by someone. "How long have you lived here?" he repeated.

Unsurprisingly, Liam simply grunted and went into his house, shutting the door firmly behind him.

Felix sighed and sat on the bench. As if sensing his disappointment, Domino bounced over to him and nuzzled his leg. He leant forward so he could pat the puppy on the head.

"It looks like you're going to be a tough nut to crack, Liam Gladstone," Felix muttered to himself. "But I will."

3

LIAM

Liam was halfway through a documentary when there was a spritely knock at his door. 'Spritely' was the only way to describe the *rat-a-tat-tat* rhythm. Liam rolled his eyes, already guessing who his late-evening visitor was.

He paused the documentary and trudged to the door, opening it.

Felix grinned at him. "Hi, neighbour."

At least Felix had stopped calling him by his full name; that was a slight bonus.

"Hello," Liam replied gruffly.

He didn't want to give off the impression that he was willing to be sociable. He wasn't. He wanted to get back to his documentary. Felix was far too cheerful to deal with for a third time in one day.

"I was wondering if I could borrow some milk?" Felix looked almost guilty as he spoke, wincing at the end of the sentence. Annoyingly, it was an endearing wince. Cute, almost.

"Milk?" Liam echoed.

"Yeah. I didn't get a chance to go shopping today, so I have nothing in the house, except puppy food. I ordered takeout for dinner, but I have no milk."

"Why do you need milk at"—Liam checked his watch—"almost ten?"

"It probably sounds stupid, but I drink warm milk before bed. It helps me sleep."

Liam raised his eyebrows. He'd been given warm milk before bedtime. When he was *five*.

"I'll replace it tomorrow," Felix offered. "If you've got any to spare, that is." He scuffed his foot against the floor and then gave Liam an utterly charmingly pleading smile.

Felix's smile was... disarming. For all that Liam wanted to roll his eyes and shake his head at the concept of a twenty-five-year-old drinking hot milk at bedtime, he couldn't. The scathing words died long before they reached his lips, leaving him staring, slightly dumb-founded, at his new neighbour. Even though the seconds dragged into at least a minute while Liam tried to gather his wits about him, Felix's smile didn't waver at all. It was unnatural, Liam decided. No one could be that unwaveringly cheerful.

"Wait there," he huffed when he was capable of speech again.

He shut the door and went to the kitchen to check what milk he had. There was no way he was letting Felix into his house. That would suggest he was welcome. He had half a bottle of full-fat milk in the fridge, which would be enough to make a mug of warm milk. It was a good thing he was due a delivery in the morning, or he wouldn't be willing to part with what he had.

When he got back to the front door, Felix was leaning against the wall. He straightened, grinning, his gaze flicking between the milk bottle and Liam's face.

"It's full fat," Liam said, holding the bottle out.

Felix accepted it, their fingertips briefly brushing. "Thanks. You get milk delivered?"

This time Liam did roll his eyes. "Yes. I would have thought that was obvious. You can't buy bottled milk in supermarkets."

Felix drew in a breath, and for a second Liam thought the boy was going to snap out a retort.

"Could I get the number so I can put an order in?" Felix asked, his voice calm and charming.

Liam narrowed his eyes. Did nothing ruffle this guy? "Wait there."

This time, he didn't shut the door as he went to a narrow table that stood in his hallway. He pulled open the drawer, sorting through business cards until he found the one for the local milkman. He copied the details onto a sheet of paper and took it to Felix.

"Thank you," Felix said politely. "That wasn't so hard, was it?"

"What?"

Felix raised his shoulders in what might have been a shrug, except he didn't lower them again. His smile morphed into a nervous grin. "Being nice?"

Liam glowered at him.

Felix dropped his shoulders. "Sorry, low blow. I really am grateful for the milk and the number. Goodnight, neighbour." He turned and walked halfway down the drive before pausing and turning. "Hey, can I get you anything tomorrow? From the shops," he added quickly. "I'll probably do an internet order."

"No."

"If you change your mind, let me know." Felix waved the hand that was clutching the piece of paper. "Night."

Rather than shutting the door, Liam watched as Felix returned to his house. He told himself he was making sure the pest was really going, but he couldn't deny that he was *also* noticing how tight Felix's jeans were on his arse. As Felix reached his door, he glanced over at Liam and grinned. Again. Didn't the man ever get tired of smiling? He must have had bionic cheek muscles. It was the only explanation.

When Felix had gone inside, Liam closed his door and went back to his documentary. Almost as soon as he'd unpaused it, his mind started wandering. If Felix had no food in the house, what was he going to eat for breakfast? Liam was a firm believer in the saying that breakfast was the most important meal of the day. It was probably because he'd had to skip lunch more times than he'd been able to grab it when he was working, first on the beat, and then as a detective. Criminals didn't care whether police officers had managed to eat or not, so he'd always loaded up on a massive breakfast before going on shift. His habits hadn't changed since he'd taken early retirement.

He tutted at himself. Felix wasn't his problem. He didn't care whether the boy starved or not. He turned up the volume on the television to drown out his thoughts. Not that it really helped, and he turned it down fairly quickly, not wanting to bother his new neighbour. He only hoped that Felix would show *him* the same consideration, although he doubted it. It was only a matter of time before Felix's playboy lifestyle became evident. There would be people over constantly. Parties. Loud music. If Felix thought a sweet smile and polite charm would make up for all that, he had another think coming.

Liam's morning routine was the same as it had always been—wake early, do one hundred press-ups, shower, have breakfast—except that Felix kept breaking into his thoughts whenever his stomach grumbled that it was hungry. It wasn't his fault that Felix hadn't bothered to go and buy food yesterday. It wasn't his problem that the boy would go hungry until he sorted himself out and went shopping. It was clear, from his limited interaction with his new neighbour, that he was an unorganised disaster with a beautiful smile. Scowling, Liam scrubbed that final thought from his mind. Or at least he tried to.

He had barely begun to organise breakfast when guilt tugged at his gut. Guilt! Why should he feel guilty for enjoying his breakfast, just because Felix would have none? The boy wasn't his responsibility. Although if Felix were *his* boy, he would make sure he took care of himself.

What was he thinking? Felix wasn't his boy and never would be. Even with that thought hanging solidly in his mind, he still found himself frying an extra egg and grilling extra bacon and sausages. He ended up consoling himself with the thought that it was the neighbourly thing to do, yet he still grumbled about his stupidity under his breath as he flipped the eggs and turned the bacon and sausages. What if Felix was like a stray dog? If he fed him once, he might keep coming back with those green puppy dog eyes to ask for one favour after another.

Liam berated himself. He was making assumptions based on limited information. In truth, he had no clue what Felix was really like. Then again, he'd made a career out of weighing people up pretty much instantly. He'd developed a gut instinct about people, and he was rarely wrong. If his intuition was screaming that Felix was a hot mess, he was ninety-nine per cent sure he was right.

He plated up both breakfasts and covered one with foil, putting it back under the grill to keep warm while he ate his own. There was no chance he was letting his food go cold while he delivered breakfast to Felix. He had meant to take his time, as he always did. He sat outside in the garden, with the rich scent of his roses and the twitter of birds to keep him company. He had a bird feeder, which was currently being used by half a dozen blue tits. Butterflies and bees had already gathered around the roses, collecting nectar. It was beautiful and peaceful, and yet he stuffed his breakfast down his face quickly, worrying that the food he'd put aside would become unpalatable. There was nothing worse than a fried egg that had gone cold and rubbery.

He was still grumbling to himself about how ridiculous he was being when he knocked on Felix's door. The plate was still warm from being under the grill, but the food definitely wouldn't be steaming hot anymore. He stood and waited, muttering under his breath about being kept waiting.

He was about to give up when the door opened and a very sleepy-looking Felix blinked at him.

"Oh, hi, neighbour," Felix said, a half smile breaking to brighten up his face.

His dark hair was dishevelled and sticking up at all kinds of crazy angles. He had sleep dust in the corners of his eyes and a light covering of stubble on his chin and jaw, but what Liam really took note of was that Felix was wearing a red satin dressing gown, which he was still in the process of tying. It ended mid-thigh, so showed off Felix's lean legs. Liam shouldn't have noticed the way the bright fabric grazed against Felix's collarbones, or the way the dressing gown wasn't fully closed at the front, revealing more than a slither of Felix's smooth, waxed chest. Nor should he have looked at Felix's legs, which were strong and willowy. But he did, and it made his mouth water. He swallowed.

"Can I help you?" Felix asked, amusement ringing in his voice.

"Breakfast," Liam said in an annoyed tone. He shoved the plate into Felix's hands. "So you don't go hungry."

"Aww," Felix said, drawing out the sound. "You do care."

"No," Liam snapped. "I don't. I had things that needed using up, that's all."

"And you thought of me." Felix's smile became wider, to the point that Liam was sure the boy's face would split in two.

The whine of Felix's puppy caught his attention, providing a welcome distraction from the half-naked man in front of him. The puppy bounded up to Felix and then sat down beside him, leaning against the young man's leg. It stared at the plate and literally licked its lips.

"Someone appreciates the smell of your cooking," Felix noted. "Sorry, little guy, this isn't for you." He yawned and wiped a hand across his face, dislodging the sleep dust onto his cheeks. "I'll get you breakfast too. Don't worry." He crouched down to scratch the puppy's head.

The dressing gown tugged up a little, revealing even more of his thighs. With Felix's attention completely diverted by the puppy, Liam couldn't help but run his tongue over his lips. There was no denying that Felix was beautiful.

Felix stood tall again. "Thank you," he said in a warm tone. "If there's ever anything I can do for you—"

"There won't be," Liam interjected. What could this haphazard young man possibly offer him? "Goodbye."

"Bye, grumpy bear," Felix said.

Although the words made Liam bristle with annoyance, he couldn't ignore the cheerfully affectionate way in which Felix said them. Even so, he hunched his shoulders and muttered about how absurd a nickname it was all the way back to his house. He wasn't grumpy. He just didn't want his quiet life to be interrupted by his new neighbour. Was that really too much to ask?

FELIX

The gate at the end of Felix's garden led to a public footpath that followed the edge of the fields. After eating the breakfast Liam had brought him, Felix took Domino for a short walk down the footpath. He kept the puppy on the lead, not wanting to lose him before he'd had a chance to train him. Not that he had a clue about doing that. He'd need to get someone to help, and he found himself idly wondering how much of a stir he'd cause by turning up at local dog training classes.

He was about to turn around when a couple of teenage girls in school uniforms rounded the corner of the field. They were chatting and laughing, but when they saw him, one of them gave him a curious look. He smiled cheerfully at them, offering them a wave as he bent down to stroke Domino. He waited for the girls to pass, watching as they whispered to one another and kept glancing back at him. One of them had pulled a phone out and kept looking at the screen, then at him.

They stopped, had an obvious discussion, and then returned to him. One girl was reluctant, her face red as her friend tugged her along.

"Excuse me," the lead girl said, "but my friend thinks you're Felix Lee."

"Shouldn't you be in school?" he felt like a killjoy.

"We're on study leave," the girl replied. "We have an exam this afternoon."

Felix might have known that was how things were done if he'd actually been at school when he was sixteen rather than being tutored while on film sets.

"So, are you Felix Lee?" the girl asked. "I told Carly you couldn't be."

"Do you think I am?" Felix asked, standing.

The girl shrugged. "You don't look handsome enough." She showed him a picture of himself on her phone as if to prove her point.

Felix laughed and rubbed the back of his neck. "They did a good airbrushing job on me, huh?"

The girl stared at him, disbelief clouding her eyes. "*Are* you Felix Lee?"

"That's what it says on my birth certificate."

The girl gaped and then squeezed her friend's hand. "Carly has a *huge* crush on you. Would you sign her…" She faltered, looking her friend up and down. "T-shirt."

Her friend, Carly, was shaking her head wildly. She looked like she wanted the ground to swallow her up.

Felix patted his pockets. "I don't have a pen, sorry.

He really was. He'd never turned a fan down before. It occurred to him that his house was literally minutes away, and he would have a pen *somewhere* in one of the boxes, but he also knew how stupid it would be to let these girls know where he lived.

They looked visibly disappointed, but there was no easy way for Felix to make it up to them. As much as he *could* send them both an autographed photo, it would be wildly inappropriate of him to ask for their addresses. Situations like these were a minefield he'd had to learn to navigate from an early age. Luckily, Emma had been on hand to help him most of the time.

"How about a selfie?" he suggested.

Emma would probably have a fit about him posing for photos outside of an organised event, especially so close to where he was living. The girls would probably tell their friends and splash the photo all over social media. It didn't necessarily bother him if people found out where he'd moved to—it would happen eventually —but he doubted Liam would want teenagers or photographers camping out on the doorstep.

"*Really?*"

Carly became animated all of a sudden and rubbed at her cheeks, like she was trying to brush the heat away from them. It didn't work, but she came and stood on one side of him. Her friend stood on the other side of Felix, and he looped his arms over their shoulders while she raised her phone. He put on his best smile as the girl took several shots.

"Just in case any of us were blinking," she said, even though she'd blatantly changed her pose and facial expression between each photo.

"No worries," Felix said jovially. "I'd better get this little rascal home."

He stooped to stroke Domino again, to a chorus of 'aww' from the girls, as though they'd just noticed the puppy for the first time. He half expected them to ask for more photos, with Domino, but they didn't. He picked the puppy up and walked in the direction he'd been going, *away* from his house. As he'd suspected, the girls didn't move at first, but by the time he'd got to the bend, they had moved off, chatting and looking at the bold girl's phone.

Felix let out a sigh. Interacting with fans was both fun and exhausting, and he'd rarely had to do it without Emma in tow. He walked a little farther, still carrying Domino before deciding the girls would be long gone and it would be okay to turn around again.

When he got back to his garden, Liam was outside, checking his roses.

"Hi, neighbour," Felix called cheerfully before bending to take the harness off Domino so the puppy could run around the garden.

Liam grunted a reply, which was oddly welcome after Felix's encounter with the girls.

"Do you check the roses every day?" he asked, jumping onto the bench again. He folded his arms across the top of the fence and then rested his chin on his hands.

"Yes."

"Huh. I never knew roses took so much looking after."

Liam glanced at him, eyes narrowed.

"I've washed your plate. Let me go get it."

Felix hopped down from the fence and let himself

into the house so he could grab the plain white plate from the draining board. He returned to the bench, as it was easier to hand the plate to Liam if he could actually see him.

"Breakfast was lovely, thank you." He should probably have said that first, but there wasn't anything he could do about it now.

Liam barely acknowledged him as he put the plate down on the patio table before going back to his roses.

Felix rested his chin on his hands again as he watched Liam work. He loved the look of fierce concentration on the big man's face and the way the sun picked out the auburn strands in his hair and beard and highlighted the curves of his bulky muscles.

"You'll need to buy a lawnmower," Liam said suddenly.

Felix blinked and lifted his head. "Sorry?"

"For your lawn," Liam said, as though Felix was a young child that needed things spelled out for him.

"Oh, yeah, good point. It's on my list of things to do." He chuckled. "I have a *huge* list."

Liam glanced at him, eyebrows pinching together.

"It would be shorter if you could recommend a decorator I could call."

Liam turned his back and carried on with what he had been doing. Felix watched, finding the man spellbinding despite his grumpy nature. A couple of minutes later, Liam marched into the house without saying goodbye.

Felix sighed and shrugged before turning and dropping down to sit on the bench. He called Domino to him and stroked the puppy's head. Domino yawned and stretched before flopping down over Felix's foot, falling asleep almost instantly. Felix laughed and leant back, clasping his hands behind his head as he soaked up the sunshine. He didn't mind not being able to move, for a little while at least.

He wasn't sure how long he'd been sitting there when a shadow fell over him. He looked up. Liam was holding a piece of paper out to him over the fence.

"The number of the decorator I used," Liam muttered. "It took me a while to find it."

Felix's mouth curled into a smile as he plucked the paper from Liam's hand.

"I'll mow your lawn for you," Liam told him. "Until you get your own lawnmower. Just make sure the puppy isn't in the garden when I do."

"I can do that," Felix assured him. "You like taking care of people, don't you?"

"No," Liam huffed.

"Okay, neighbour," Felix said, his agreement about as convincing as Liam's denial had been.

"I don't," Liam said more firmly.

Felix turned so it was easier to look up at Liam, dislodging the puppy, who whined and then went straight back to sleep. "Maybe it's just me you like taking care of," he joked. It was only once he'd said it that he realised that concept made him feel warm inside.

"Don't be ridiculous," Liam muttered.

Felix stood and stepped back onto the bench, giving himself a height advantage. Liam took a step back and folded his arms. When he did that, the veins in his arms popped, and his massive muscles bulged, making Felix's legs feel like jelly. What would it feel like to be wrapped up in that embrace? Felix dismissed the thought, or at least, he tried to, but it was pretty damn hard when Liam was right there, almost within touching distance.

"So you don't think I need taking care of?" Felix teased, tilting his head to the side.

"I didn't say that," Liam said, his voice lowering to a growl.

Felix doubted it was meant to sound sexy, but it was.

"Oh," Felix said, nodding in understanding. "So I *do* need taking care of?"

Liam shook his head. "You're annoying," he accused.

"I try."

Liam rolled his eyes. "And insufferable."

"Really?"

"Yes. Completely and utterly unbearable." With that, Liam stomped inside.

Felix laughed and sat down, turning his face up to the sun again. Seconds later, he heard the soft scrape of a window being opened.

"Put some sun cream on before you burn," Liam called from the upstairs window.

Felix chuckled quietly to himself. Liam *did* care, on some level at least. That was good to know.

5

LIAM

"Now who could that be?" Liam grumbled as someone knocked at his door, even though he already knew who it was.

He hadn't ordered anything, and none of his family had arranged to visit him, which left Felix. What did the irritating boy want now?

It didn't surprise him to find Felix smiling up at him as he opened the door, but the bag of delicious-smelling food was unexpected.

"Hi, neighbour," Felix said, as cheerfully as ever. "I've got a confession to make." He blushed and dipped his chin. "It turns out, you can't get same-day delivery from the supermarket, *but* I did manage to snag a slot for tomorrow." He grinned as though he had just won at adulting.

Liam was *not* impressed.

"But it means I'm still out of milk," Felix went on a little sheepishly. "So I was hoping to trade food for some more." He lifted up the bag. "I hope you like

Indian. I got plenty for two, although I had to guess at what you might like."

Liam's eyes bugged at Felix's audacity.

"Can I come in?" Felix asked, his smile not wavering for a second.

"Do you always smile so much?" Liam asked because he was too gobsmacked to send the boy home.

"I guess so."

"It's insufferable."

"So you said before," Felix reminded him.

Liam growled.

"Are you always so grumpy?" Felix asked, his tone teasing.

Liam glowered at him. He hadn't forgotten Felix calling him a 'grumpy bear' that morning.

"I like grumpy," Felix told him. "Are you going to invite me in?" He shrugged nonchalantly. "It's cool if you don't want to. Take whatever food you want, and I'll take the rest home to eat. *Alone*." He said the last word mournfully, pouting slightly, his eyes going all puppy dog again.

Goddamn, but it made Liam want to invite the boy in.

"You want milk?" he asked.

"In exchange for food. Have you already eaten?"

"No." Liam realised his mistake as Felix's smile became bright again, like sunshine. "That's not the point," he blustered. "You've got no right swanning over here, inviting yourself in."

"I was hoping you'd do the inviting."

Felix looked so unbelievably endearing, which left

Liam spluttering as he tried to make his mouth tell Felix to leave. Of course, that didn't happen, because he literally couldn't form the words. He mentally cursed his body for betraying him. There was no reason to let Felix in and yet…

"Come in," he said through gritted teeth.

Felix's smile turned into a triumphant one as Liam stepped aside, letting him in.

"Is your kitchen at the back, the same as mine?" Felix asked.

He didn't wait for an answer, just wandered confidently through the house to the kitchen. By the time Liam had shut the door, Felix had found bowls and cutlery and was in the middle of opening up the cartons of takeaway. It smelt amazing. Liam's stomach agreed, growling noisily.

"Do you mind if we eat outside?" Felix asked. "I noticed you have a table, and it's still pretty warm."

It was hot outside, with no breeze to cool the air down. The evening sunlight had a soft quality to it as it brushed the very edge of the garden.

Again, Felix didn't wait for an answer. He simply started to ferry things out the back door to the table.

"Could you grab drinks?"

Liam's mouth opened and closed a few times. He wasn't used to being ordered around, especially by a young upstart like Felix. It made him want to take charge and lay down some demands of his own. He took a breath. Felix *had* asked. It hadn't been an instruction, even though it had briefly felt like one. Clearly, the boy wasn't used to people telling him 'no', adding more fuel to

Liam's theory that he was a useless playboy. After pouring them both a glass of water, he joined Felix outside.

"I got us chicken Tikka Jalfrezi, lamb Rogan Josh, and plenty of naan bread." Felix glanced at him, eyebrows raised ever so slightly in a manner that suggested he was seeking approval for his choices.

"Fine," Liam said grudgingly. "I like both."

"Great!" Felix served them a generous dollop of both and then tore a naan bread in two, handing half to Liam before tucking into his food heartily.

By the way he ate, it looked like he hadn't eaten all day. Well, since breakfast anyway. Liam realised he probably hadn't, as he still wouldn't have any food in the house.

"You shouldn't skip lunch," he berated, even though he'd made a career out of it.

Or maybe he'd said it *because* he'd done it so often himself. He knew how off his game being hungry could make him.

Felix paused, staring at him for a few seconds before cracking a smile. "I won't make a habit of it, I promise."

Liam couldn't tell if the boy was taking the piss or not, so he glowered at Felix to be on the safe side.

"It's my turn," Felix said, seemingly at random.

"Your turn…?" Liam began, not having a clue what Felix was talking about.

"To ask you questions."

"No."

Felix pinched his lips together. "Why?"

"It's none of your business."

"What isn't?"

Liam made a hopeless gesture. "Anything. *Everything.*"

Felix dipped a piece of naan bread in his sauce. "I get it. You're the strong and silent type." He munched on the sauce-drenched bread. "A lot of guys would find that sexy," he said matter-of-factly once he'd swallowed the food down.

Liam ground his teeth because it was the only way to stop himself from asking if Felix found it sexy. "No," he said instead. "I just value my privacy."

"Unlike me?" Felix asked, raising his eyebrows.

Liam snorted. "*I'm* not the one who transported an uncovered six-foot-tall painting of a nude man pleasuring himself."

Felix chuckled. "I'm glad you appreciated my painting."

Liam felt his face growing hot. He hated that Felix was able to annoy him so easily. He didn't normally rise to bait or walk into traps of his own making.

"You realise it's not fair that I know *nothing* about you?" Felix said. "Except your name, that you like to grow roses, and that you're a grumpy bear."

Liam felt like slapping his hand over his face, although he managed to stop himself.

"Do you work?" Felix asked.

Liam sighed heavily. Felix was going to keep asking questions, and refusing to answer would only make him look churlish.

"I'm retired."

Felix's eyes widened. "Really? You don't look old enough."

"I took early retirement."

"Why?" Felix popped another piece of naan bread into his mouth.

"Because I wanted to," Liam snapped.

"Fair," Felix mused. "I'm taking a career break."

"You work?"

Felix laughed loudly, right from his belly. "There's no need to sound so surprised."

"I…" Liam glared at his bowl. "Assumed you were a playboy."

"A playboy?" Felix laughed even harder. His knee knocked into the table, rattling everything on it. "Why?"

"Your furniture. The bar. That painting."

"My, my, you *were* being a nosey neighbour yesterday," Felix teased. "I'm an actor."

Liam wondered if he was supposed to be impressed by that.

"I've had a pretty hectic schedule over the last couple of years, so I decided to take some time off."

"Buying a house is taking time off?" Liam asked incredulously.

"A house and a puppy."

Liam was more confused than ever by Felix. He made buying a house and a dog sound as casual as popping to the supermarket.

"So you won't be having any wild parties?"

Felix shrugged. "I'm not planning any." He pushed his empty bowl away. "I don't think Domino would like the noise." His smile became lop-sided, and he met Liam's stare, his green eyes sparkling.

He was teasing Liam again. Naughty boy. Felix needed more than looking after, but Liam kept that thought to himself.

"What did you do?" Felix asked.

"I was a detective constable."

"Wow! Really? Like Sherlock Holmes or were you more like Poirot? Did you solve lots of cases? You must have solved tons."

Liam waved his hands for Felix to slow down.

"I bet you were amazing at it," Felix said. "I mean, you had me figured out after knowing me for a couple of days." He waggled his eyebrows.

Liam puffed out an annoyed breath.

"I'm sorry," Felix said. "I don't mean to tease."

"Yes, you do," Liam snapped.

Felix rested his chin on his hand and gazed into Liam's eyes. "You're right, I do. A little." He traced a circle on the table with his finger. "No offence, but I didn't think police officers got paid that much, not even detective constables. Plus, don't you have to be seventy-five to retire?"

"Are you always this nosey?"

Felix grinned. "Yes."

Liam sighed.

"Police officers can retire at fifty with a basic pension, as long as they have twenty-five years' service."

Felix's face slackened slightly. "You don't look fifty."

"I'm not. I deferred my pension until I am."

"So… If you're not getting your pension yet, what

are you living on? Fresh air and roses?"

Liam was fed up of being interrogated, but apparently Felix wasn't going to shut up until he had some answers.

"I never married, and I don't have kids. I worked in central London and didn't splash money around on flashy sports cars or six-foot paintings of nude men."

"Good burn," Felix said approvingly. "Carry on."

Liam glowered at him. "Between money I'd put away and the sale of my flat, I was able to afford to buy this place and have enough money to live off until I can draw my pension."

Felix whistled. "Your flat must have been crazy expensive."

"It was in London," Liam said sardonically. "I live in the northeast now. House prices are *much* lower up here."

Felix glanced around. "And I guess living like a boring old hermit helps."

Without giving Liam a chance to grumble at him or cuff him around the ear—which Liam was sorely tempted to do to punish the boy for his impishness—Felix began to clear the plates and takeaway cartons. After picking them all up, he went into the kitchen. Liam was able to watch the boy through the open door as he washed up.

He had decided that Felix was bewildering. Unfortunately, he was also bewitching, and Liam couldn't make himself look away. It didn't help that Felix's back was to him and that, yet again, he was wearing jeans that were tight around his arse. Of course, the brain in his dick started talking louder than the brain in his head, and he found himself imagining cupping that arse in his hands, squeezing it, and maybe even spanking it.

He tore his stare away from Felix and forced himself to look at his roses instead. It had been too long since he'd felt another man's bare skin against his own. Frustration and lust were conspiring to make him look at Felix with infatuation. How could he want to be with someone who infuriated him so much? How could he want to touch him, taste him, and put him in his place —*if* he was willing? His cock swelled, forcing him to turn his body towards the garden to hide it.

"I should go," Felix said from behind him, a short time later.

Liam grunted, still unable to turn around. Felix had already decided he was grumpy. He might as well play into that impression; it was certainly better than revealing that he had a hard-on.

There was a pause before Felix said, "Goodnight, Liam."

Liam's eyes widened. It was the first time Felix had called him Liam. Not Liam Gladstone. Not neighbour or grumpy bear, just Liam. His name sounded nice, spoken in Felix's soft, smoky voice, making him want to hear it again.

He cleared his throat, which was thick with lust. "Goodnight." It came out gruffly.

It was several minutes after Felix had gone before Liam's hard-on had subsided, and he remembered the boy had wanted to trade dinner for milk, and Liam had let him go home empty-handed.

6

FELIX

Felix's day was filled with calls and using his phone as a hotspot so he could use the internet on his laptop. He managed to arrange for a number of tradesmen to visit over the next few days in order to give him quotes for decorating, new flooring, extending the patio, and a new bathroom and kitchen. He also ordered a lawnmower and an outdoor table and chairs. The house needed new curtains and blinds too, but that wasn't something he could organise until the house was decorated. He wondered if it would be too extravagant to hire an interior designer to take charge for him; it would certainly make his life easier and take a lot of the decision-making and worry out of his hands. By the time he was done, he was mentally tired. Who knew that having your own house could be so exhausting? It was the worst time for Emma to call, so of course she did.

"Hi, Emma," he said.

"I've been trying to reach you all day," she told him.

"I've been busy."

She couldn't have been trying for long, as she lived in LA, so wouldn't even have been up for long.

Felix put the phone onto speaker mode and set it down on the kitchen worktop, as he made a sandwich. He'd skipped breakfast and lunch while waiting for his food delivery and was now starving but too tired to care about cooking properly. Outside, he could hear the buzz of a lawnmower.

"Apparently so," Emma said curtly. "How's the quiet life?"

Felix chuckled as he laid a thick slice of beef onto the bread he'd just buttered. "Not so quiet today."

"I'm surprised you're not bored already."

Felix paused. He hadn't really had time to be bored. Before moving in, he'd been staying with his long-term friend, Rick. They'd spent their time catching up, trying to train Domino, and furniture-shopping. Since he'd moved in, he'd been busy organising things and verbally sparring with Liam. If anything, time had been slipping away faster than he'd expected.

"The quiet life has its charms," he mused, thinking of his grumpy bear of a neighbour.

He glanced down as Domino nuzzled his ankle. The puppy stared at him with wide eyes.

"You've had your food," he told him. "This is mine."

"I've got a script for you," Emma said. "You'll love it."

"Emma…" Felix took a breath. "I thought we agreed no scripts for now?"

"We did, but you can't blame a girl for trying. You should be flattered, Felix. Casting directors want *you*."

"I am flattered," he assured her as he cut a tomato and added the slices to the sandwich. "But I also need a break."

"It'll be months before they start filming. You'll still get your time off."

He sliced some cucumber next, added lettuce, and then spread a generous dollop of mustard to the other slice of bread before squishing the whole sandwich down and cutting it in half so it was easier to pick up in one hand.

"Felix?"

"I'm making some food."

"You've also got me on speaker. I can tell, you know."

"What do you want me to say?" He took a bite of the sandwich, which tasted amazing after a day of not eating.

"That you'll at least read the script. That's all I'm asking, Felix. Read it. You might love it."

"I thought you said I *would* love it?"

"You will."

"Fine," Felix breathed. "Send it over." He'd never been able to say no to her.

"You won't regret it." Excitement made Emma's voice bubbly.

"I'm not promising anything," Felix warned her.

"I know you, Felix," she stated. "You will love it, and you'll be back on a film set before you know it. You only think you want a break, but you're going to miss this life sooner than you think. You'll find the novelty of going at a slower pace will wear off quickly, and you'll thank me for having a film lined up when it does."

"You might be right," Felix said warily.

"I *am* right. I'll get it sent by courier. You'll have it in the next couple of days. Read it and let me know what you think. Let me know if there's anything you need."

"I will."

After Emma had hung up, Felix went out to the garden and sat on the bench in the late afternoon sunlight. Domino bounded after him, probably still hopeful of receiving a tidbit. Behind him, the sound of Liam mowing his lawn filled the air. They hadn't spoken since the previous night. The temptation rose in Felix to stand on the bench and say hi, but he didn't. There had been a weird tension in the air when he'd left Liam's house last night. Liam had been even grumpier than usual, not even deigning to look at Felix to say goodnight. It had stung a bit, but Felix was doing his best to shrug it off. He *had* gatecrashed Liam's evening. Besides, if he stayed quiet, he could imagine Liam mowing the lawn, preferably topless.

He'd just finished his sandwich when the lawnmower stopped. Seconds later, a shadow fell over him, prompting him to look up.

"Hi, neighbour," he said, beaming up at Liam.

Liam's face glistened with a thin sheen of sweat. "I want to mow your lawn."

His authoritative tone made Felix shiver. "I'll get Domino out of the way."

Plate in hand, he urged the puppy into the house and shut him inside. He went back to the bench, lying down, with his hands tucked behind his head.

"Comfortable?" Liam asked in his usual gruff tone as he let himself into the garden.

"Yup. Do you need me to plug the lawnmower in?"

"It's cordless," Liam retorted.

Felix wondered if he should have bought a cordless one. He hadn't really thought about it when he'd been looking online. It wasn't like he'd ever used one or had to take care of his own lawn before.

He pretended to doze while really watching Liam methodically cut the grass, his mouth practically watering at the way the man's muscles moved as he pushed the lawnmower back and forth. He couldn't help but think that Liam would be cooler if he took his top off.

When he'd finished, Liam came and stood in exactly the right way to block the sunlight from warming Felix's body.

"Done," he announced.

"Thank you," Felix said sincerely. "Does that mean I'm forgiven?"

"For what?"

"Bugging you last night."

Liam's nostrils flared, but he didn't reply.

"Maybe not." Felix sat upright. "What can I do to make it up to you?"

"Be less annoying?"

"I'm not sure that's possible. I could get you a drink," Felix suggested instead. "The shopping arrived."

"Well done," Liam said sarcastically. "What does it feel like to be an adult?"

Felix stretched his legs out, pretending to contemplate the question. "Not all it's cracked up to be. It's kind of exhausting, actually."

Liam huffed. "Says the guy who's been lounging around while *I* do all the hard work."

"It was tiring watching you."

Liam curled his upper lip and then shook his head.

"Drink?" Felix offered again. "Or maybe a cold flannel?"

"No, thanks."

Liam went to retrieve the lawnmower.

"Would you tell me about your roses?" Felix asked, following him out of his garden into Liam's.

"No."

"I'm not teasing you," Felix assured him. "I want to know. I didn't know so many different types of roses existed. Please?"

"No," Liam snapped. He put the lawnmower away in the shed.

Felix decided to give up, for the time being. He'd whittle Liam down slowly because he really was curious about the roses.

"You obviously love gardening," he said, slowly shuffling towards the greenhouse. "Would you at least show me what's in here?" He opened the door and darted inside before Liam could utter a word.

The big man followed him, moving surprisingly quickly for such a heavily built guy. The greenhouse was oppressively hot. Tables with trays containing dozens of plant pots filled most of the space, though there was room to walk around and reach every pot. Some of the pots were empty. Others had little plants in them. Felix had no clue what they were. Baby roses, maybe?

"Get out," Liam growled.

Felix turned to face him, tilting his chin up. "Why?" He widened his eyes. "Are you hiding something illegal in here? Are you a secret drug lord?"

Liam's face turned stormy, which was actually pretty frightening. "No."

"Then what's the harm?" Felix gestured to the pots. "They're just plants."

Liam rubbed at his temples with his forefingers. "You are infuriating," he spat out through his teeth.

"Yes," Felix agreed. "But that's why you like me."

"I don't like you," Liam told him. "You annoy me."

"Everyone likes me," Felix said, batting his eyelids and putting on his brightest smile. "It just takes some people longer to realise that they do. You'll get there."

Liam continued to glower at him. Maybe Felix had gone a step too far.

"I'm sorry for offending you, grumpy bear. I'll go."

He slipped past Liam so he could leave the greenhouse.

"I used to be a detective," Liam reminded him.

Felix stopped in his tracks and turned to face him.

"I've dealt with dirty cops," Liam told him. "I'm not one."

Which was why Felix had struck a raw nerve.

"The law is important to you?" Felix asked, perhaps a little stupidly.

Liam nodded. "*Rules* are very important to me."

The hairs on Felix's arms rose at Liam's words, and his stomach quivered. "Maybe you should set me some rules to follow," he said a little breathlessly. He wasn't even sure where the suggestion had come from, but his mouth kept talking while his brain scrabbled to catch up. "Teach me how to behave."

Liam's eyes grew wide. "Is that what you want?" His voice was strained but not as severe as it had been seconds earlier.

Felix shrugged. "Maybe it's what I need." He caught his breath, his chest tightening as he watched Liam carefully.

The grumpy bear did nothing but stare back at him. Silence stretched between them, and for a few seconds, Felix became hyperaware of all the other sensations around him. Of the scent of the roses that was making him feel a little light-headed. The plethora of birds, clamouring for a spot at the bird feeder. Domino yapping from next door. The kiss of the breeze against his skin. Despite all that, he was able to focus in on Liam. Like him, Liam seemed to be holding his breath. His fists were loosely clenched, his body was stiff, his expression unreadable.

"Rule number one," Liam said in a low but commanding voice.

Felix tapped his fingers against his thigh as he waited for him to continue.

"Don't wind me up."

Felix pouted. "But it's so easy," he whined. "And so much fun."

Liam raised his hand, which instantly silenced Felix. "Rule number two. Don't answer back."

Felix pressed his lips together to prevent himself from making a glib response.

"Now go," Liam said, pointing towards the back gate. "You're exhausting."

"I thought I was infuriating and insufferable?"

Liam glared at him. "Do I need to get you to repeat rule number two?"

"Don't answer back," Felix said with a grin. "I've got it. Bye, grumpy bear."

He felt light as he left Liam's garden, his heart practically skipping with excitement. He wasn't entirely sure what had just happened, but it had been oddly exhilarating, and he wanted it to happen again.

7

LIAM

Liam couldn't get the greenhouse incident out of his head. To be more accurate, he couldn't get Felix out of his head. He couldn't decide if Felix's request for rules had been sexually charged or not, but it sure as hell had felt like it. He'd had to send the boy away because his body wanted to react, and he couldn't let it in front of Felix while maintaining his stern composure. Luckily, Felix had done as he was told, although that had added more fuel to the fire in Liam's groin. He'd gone inside to take a long, hot shower, beating himself off to fantasies of putting Felix on his knees in front of him. Felix would make such a good boy. He would be very naughty, but that would be half the fun.

There was no guarantee that was what Felix wanted, though. No assurance that the young man hadn't simply been innocently messing around. If he'd never been involved in the scene, he probably hadn't even realised what he'd said or how much he'd turned Liam on. The truth was, Liam had no clue what experiences Felix had had, and there was no easy way to broach the subject, not without confessing his sexual attraction for the infuriating young man. He didn't want to take that step until he was absolutely certain that Felix was interested. That Felix *wanted* him. They were neighbours, which meant they couldn't escape each other. The last thing he wanted was to make things utterly intolerable between them by making unreciprocated advances.

He tried to push Felix out of his mind throughout the afternoon but couldn't manage it. Thoughts of the young man seeped into every part of his being. It was pure lust and perhaps a craving to have a boy in his life again, if only for a few hours.

Once the sun started to go down, he ventured outside to water the roses. Relaxing music drifted over the fence from Felix's garden. Long, soft notes with bird song in the background. Liam knew he should bite down his curiosity and do what he'd come out to do, but he couldn't. He wanted to know what Felix was up to.

When he peered over the fence, he saw Felix on a long blue yoga mat. The boy had his back to the fence and was kneeling on the floor, his bare feet tucked under his bottom. His forehead rested against the floor, as were his outstretched arms. He was wearing a pair of loose-fitting jogging bottoms. The dying rays of the sun bathed Felix's bare back in golden light. Liam's mouth watered at the sight. He made up his mind to walk away, but his feet remained rooted to the spot. Warmth flowed through his body, pooling in his groin.

Slowly, Felix pushed up so his back was slightly arched and his thighs were a perfect vertical line. Liam couldn't name any poses, but he knew Felix was doing yoga. Something else he hadn't known about the boy; probably just one item in a very long list.

In one slow, graceful movement, Felix pushed forward onto his arms, his back and legs a long, flowing line to his pointed toes. He straightened one leg and raised the other into the air. His arms and torso formed one side of a V, the leg he was resting his weight on the other side. Was the blood rushing to his head while he was effectively upside down? Would it make him dizzy?

Felix moved into a low lunge. He was incredibly supple. Liam couldn't even imagine being able to do a single one of those poses, but Felix made it look effortless. He stood, one leg forward, knee bent, with his arms stretched to the sky. His back looked soft and kissable. The jogging bottoms sat low on his body, revealing the tops of his hips. Felix bent over and put his hands flat on the floor, which stretched the jogging bottoms tight over his arse. It was a glorious sight.

"Hi, neighbour," Felix said, amusement ringing in his voice.

Liam practically jumped out of his skin. Felix must have been peeking through his legs. How else could he have known Liam was there?

Liam put on his surliest glare. "I came to see what the racket was," he snapped.

"You don't like my music?" Felix asked, standing, turning, and stretching.

"No." Dear God, that wasn't true. If that music was

always accompanied by such a beautiful show, he would happily listen to it daily. "What were you doing?"

"Yoga. Want to try?"

"Don't be ridiculous."

Felix laughed. "You might like it."

"I doubt it."

"It's relaxing," Felix assured him.

The boy rolled his shoulders and tilted his head from side to side, then turned off the music before wandering up to the fence. He came as close as he could, gripping the top of the fence with his hands as he grinned at Liam.

"Did you enjoy watching me?" Felix's eyes sparkled, and his voice was lower and huskier than normal.

"I already told you—"

"You'd come to tell me to turn off the music. I understand."

Liam tried to read Felix. *Was* he flirting, or was it all a silly game to him? Briefly, Liam thought about backtracking and admitting that he had, in fact, been watching Felix. It was probably obvious that he had been anyway, so why deny it? Why not put his lust out into the open?

He couldn't bring himself to do it.

"Was there anything else?" Felix asked, eyebrows lifting slightly.

"Just keep the music down next time," Liam huffed.

"Will do, grumpy bear."

Liam drew his eyebrows down into a scowl.

Felix stared at him for a long moment, and then his eyes widened as though he'd just had a lightbulb moment. "Does calling you grumpy bear count as winding you up?"

"Yes."

"Oh." Felix looked visibly disappointed. "But it suits you."

Liam growled deep in his throat. "If you want me to set you rules, I expect you to follow them."

Felix sighed dramatically. "No calling you grumpy bear." Although his sly smile suggested that he'd be calling Liam that in his head, even if he didn't say the words out loud.

"Has anyone ever taught you to behave before?" Liam asked, taking a risk.

"Do you mean my parents?"

Liam cleared his throat. That wasn't what he'd meant, but Felix's innocent answer told him he needed to back off.

"Yes, your parents."

"I didn't have a lot of boundaries growing up," Felix admitted. "I was on set a lot, away from my family. I had chaperones and tutors, but it's not the same."

Liam's curiosity was piqued. "How long have you been acting for?" He debated asking what TV shows Felix had been in, but he wouldn't have heard of any of them, let alone have watched them.

"Mum started me in modelling when I was a baby. Clothes," Felix added. "I did a lot of catalogues. I landed my first acting gig when I was eight."

Liam whistled softly. Felix was twenty-five, which meant he'd been acting for seventeen years. He wasn't sure if he was impressed at the boy's dedication or if he felt sorry for him. From the sounds of it, Felix's childhood had been far from normal, so it was no wonder he lacked discipline, was haphazard, and overconfident. He really did need taking in hand.

It was fascinating finding out more about Felix, but it wasn't helping Liam gauge if the boy was interested in him or if he had any experience with kink at all.

Felix stretched and yawned. "I should probably take a shower and get some food. Do you want to join me?"

Liam had to clench his teeth to stop his mouth falling open.

"For dinner," Felix clarified. "I have no clue what I'm going to make, and I'm not a good cook…"

"You're not selling the offer," Liam muttered.

"Maybe I'm hoping you'll offer to cook for me," Felix said.

Liam folded his arms and gave Felix a stern look.

"No?"

"No."

"I guess I was wrong," Felix said.

"About what?"

"You, wanting to take care of me."

"I don't." Oh, but he did. So, so much, just not in the way Felix was suggesting.

"I bet that you'll be cooking me dinner before the week is out," Felix declared.

"And why would I do that?"

Felix shrugged. "Because you like me."

"I already told you—"

"That you *don't* like me. I know. You keep saying that, but I'm just not buying it."

"You're teasing me again," Liam snapped.

"I am?" Felix gasped, the sound fake. "Well, aren't I naughty?" He pinched his lower lip with his teeth as he began to back away from the fence in the direction of his back door. "Bye, grumpy—" He put his hand over his mouth. "There I go, doing it again." He grinned and then turned on his heel. "Good evening, Liam Gladstone," he called over his shoulder. "Enjoy dinner. Without me."

When Liam was sure Felix was gone, he allowed himself to smile. *If* Felix ever wanted to play, he would certainly be a handful.

8

FELIX

For all his teasing, Felix was confused about where the conversation with Liam had gone wrong. He flopped onto the purple sofa, one hand resting over his stomach, the other absently stroking Domino, who had followed him into the sitting room. The one thing he'd set up was the TV, but he hadn't organised getting it hooked up to a satellite or cable service yet, so he was left with the channels you could get through a TV aerial. He stared at the screen, not really watching, as he tried to unpick what he'd done wrong.

He was used to dissecting his performances, to see where he'd failed to hit the mark and what he needed to improve on, but this was different. He felt like he was missing something, but he wasn't sure what. Maybe Rick would know.

He reached for his phone, found Rick in his contacts, and hit the dial button.

"Felix!" Rick exclaimed as he answered the phone. "How's it going? Enjoying country life?"

"I haven't been here long enough to know," Felix admitted. "But I like what I've seen so far."

He liked being able to go on a peaceful walk, straight out of his back gate, and looked forward to when Domino was bigger and could go farther. He liked the quiet, although he was finding it hard to get to sleep. Apparently, the constant hum of traffic and city noises had acted like a lullaby. Not that he'd known or appreciated it at the time. And, of course, there was Liam. He smiled happily, remembering Liam's adorably grouchy expression when he'd called him grumpy bear.

"Good, good," Rick said.

Felix took a breath. "I need some advice."

"Advice?" Rick didn't sound surprised.

Why would he be? Rick was one of the few constants in Felix's life. They'd known each other for years, since before his film career had really taken off and he'd stopped living anything resembling a normal life. Unlike a lot of the people he'd known, Rick hadn't become completely starstruck and had kept in touch, helping to ground Felix in reality.

"There's this guy…" Felix began.

"I might have known." Rick laughed.

Felix filled Rick in on who Liam was and what had happened between them so far. "Have I got it wrong?" he asked when he was done. "Am I assuming he fancies me because I think he's hot?"

"Go back a bit to where you were doing yoga," Rick said. "Are you sure he *was* watching you?"

"Pretty sure," Felix said. "I didn't see him until I looked through my legs, but I knew he was there." It sounded too corny to say he'd felt the big man's watchful presence. "And he did have lust in his eyes."

Rick laughed. "I'll take your word for that. Walk me through what happened."

"I teased him—"

"Typical Felix."

"—He got all grumpy and sexy and brought up his rules again." He sighed, remembering the delightful shivers that had run through his body when Liam had mentioned them, his voice all gruff, gravelly, and deliciously sexy. "Then somehow we ended up talking about my parents and my acting career."

"How?" Rick asked. "What exactly did you say?"

Felix stared at the ceiling as he tried to remember. Domino licked his fingers and nuzzled at his hand.

"Liam asked me if anyone had ever taught me to behave before, and I asked him if he meant my parents."

Rick started cackling on the other end of the phone.

"What?" Felix asked indignantly.

"Felix, I love you, but sometimes you're completely dense."

Felix frowned, confused.

"And I know you're not sweet and innocent. You've been to kink clubs, right?"

"Once or twice." He'd been to all kinds of clubs and tried all sorts of things, including stuff he regretted, like drugs.

"So you know some guys like to take charge."

"Well, yes."

"And you realise that's what Liam wants to do, right?"

"Yes." Felix thought that was pretty obvious. "And?"

Rick laughed down the phone again, the sound devolving into desperate wheezes as he obviously tried to get control of himself enough to speak. "The guy wants to turn you over his knee and spank you for being naughty," Rick said bluntly. "You *have* been spanked before, haven't you?"

"Yes," Felix mumbled.

He'd been spanked in a club by a stranger, but it had had nothing to do with being naughty. It was just what happened in the room he'd gone into, and he'd been happy to give it a go. He'd liked it.

"And then you—" Rick began laughing uncontrollably again. "—You—" He snorted and then hiccupped. "—Thought he was talking about—"

Felix drummed his fingers on his stomach impatiently.

"—About—"

"I could go off you," Felix warned.

"—Your parents! The dude probably thought you were all sweet and innocent and decided to back off."

Felix's frown deepened.

"Your neighbour is a Dom," Rick said.

Felix blinked and then smacked his forehead. "You're right. I'm dense."

"Damn right, you are. What you *should* have said is 'no, but I'd like *you* to teach me how to behave.' Assuming you do, obviously."

Felix swallowed. Was that what he wanted? He thought of the way he'd felt when Liam had given him the two rules and the way he'd chosen to flaunt them.

Had he been asking to be spanked subconsciously? A thrill ran through him, giving him his answer.

"Felix?"

"I do," he whispered, turning onto his side so he could pet Domino more easily. He sighed. "But I've screwed things up."

"Only temporarily," Rick said.

"You said it yourself. He thinks I'm inexperienced—"

"Which you are," Rick interjected.

"I'm not."

"You've had lots of sex," Rick said. "You've been to a couple of fetish clubs and been spanked. That doesn't make you well versed in all things kink."

"How do I show him I want to learn?" Felix asked. "How do I show him I want *him* to teach me?"

"And discipline you?" Rick asked.

"Yes."

"Tell him? Show him?"

"And if I'm wrong?" Felix asked. "If we're *both* wrong and he's not into me, *or* a Dom... He's my neighbour, Rick. We have to live next door to each other."

"You can ignore each other or move. If you want him, show him," Rick said. "Be aggressive, Felix. Be-e aggressive."

Felix laughed. "You're still quoting that film."

"I'm still watching it at least once a month too. Sexy cheerleaders? Yes, please."

Be aggressive. Show Liam he wanted him and everything that came with that. Felix could do that.

Felix woke early, showered, and then pulled on a pair of yoga shorts. They'd been bought for him as a joke Christmas present, by Rick funnily enough, but they'd be perfect to show Liam he wanted him. Or annoy the heck out of him and make him even grumpier, but that probably amounted to the same thing. After letting Domino out to pee, Felix grabbed his Bluetooth speakers and phone and headed out into the garden. There was no sign of Liam, so Felix decided to crank the music up as loud as it would go without his speakers distorting it. He went to the same spot on the grass that he'd used the evening before, and began the yoga sequence he enjoyed doing, beginning on the floor in the Child's Pose.

It was hard to focus on breathing and taking his time when his mind with racing with thoughts of Liam's potential reaction to the music and what he was wearing. Was it too much? Was he being too antagonistic? His heart hammered against his chest as he debated turning the music off and going back inside. He didn't. He was drawn to Liam like a moth to a flame. He wanted the man's hands on his skin and to feel Liam's lips against his own, beard and all.

He was only on the third pose when he heard Liam's back door open. Felix couldn't help but grin. He had his back to the fence, just as before. He could practically feel Liam's grumpy presence behind him, silent. Hopefully, he was watching because he was about to get an eyeful.

Felix widened his stance and leant down into the Downward Dog pose, his arse thrust high in the air. He looked through his parted legs, and sure enough, there was Liam, glaring at him over the fence.

"Hi, neighbour," he said with a cheerful grin.

"Your music's too loud," Liam barked. "And who the hell does yoga in their underwear?"

Felix bent his knees. "They're yoga shorts, not underwear. Do you like them?"

"They look ridiculous," Liam huffed.

Considering they were navy blue with bright pink hearts all over them, he could understand why Liam might think they were underwear, and yes, they were a little ridiculous.

"They're meant to feel like a second skin when you're wearing them," Felix informed Liam as he stood tall and stretched. "Great for exercising." Then he turned and sauntered towards the fence. He stopped, tilting his hips coquettishly. "You can look at the logo if you don't believe me." He grazed his fingers over the small logo, which was just above the hem on the outside of the left leg.

Liam said nothing, but his expression was stormy, and his lips twitched as though he was trying to work out what to say.

"They're form-fitting," Felix said in a lower tone. "But I'm sure you can see that. They're soft to touch…" He let his voice trail off as he stared up into Liam's eyes.

"You haven't turned the music off yet," Liam said, his voice strained.

"Do I have to?"

"Yes."

Felix folded his arms loosely. "Obeying you wasn't one of the rules you set. You told me not to wind you up and not to answer back."

"You *are* winding me up."

"Am I?" Felix lifted his eyebrows.

"You know you are," Liam grated out through clenched teeth. "Now turn the music off."

Felix didn't move. Liam stared at him angrily, but Felix was damned if he was going to back down.

"New rule," Liam said. "Do as I say."

Felix lifted his chin a little. "Why should I?"

"You're answering back," Liam said in a warning tone.

"I'm asking a question."

Liam growled and then turned from the fence, vanishing from sight. Felix's body slumped. Had he pushed too far or simply read Liam completely wrong? Either way, living next door to the grumpy bear was going to be a lot less fun.

He snapped his head round as the gate opened. Liam stalked into the garden, slamming the gate shut. He was wearing a dressing gown, pulled across his body, which reached down to his knees. He had pale blue pyjama bottoms on but, like Felix, was barefooted.

Felix stood his ground, holding his breath, as Liam marched up to him and stood a hair's breadth from him. He could feel the man's breath on his face.

"Do you want me to teach you how to behave?" Liam demanded. "Is that what this little show is all about?"

Felix nodded and then swallowed hard, unable to find his voice.

"Do you understand what that means?" Liam asked.

"I think so." Felix realised he was trembling. Not from fear but from anticipation and excitement.

"Rule number one?"

"Don't tease you," Felix whispered.

"Two?"

"Don't answer back."

"Three?"

"Do as you say."

Liam pointed to the speakers. "Turn the music off."

Felix obeyed instantly and then returned to where he'd been standing.

Liam reached out and pinged the waistband of Felix's yoga shorts. "These are ridiculous," he snarled.

"But they got your attention," Felix pointed out. "Or you wouldn't be standing here now."

"*You* got my attention," Liam said.

Felix's knees felt week. "By being naughty?" he asked playfully.

"You are very naughty," Liam agreed, his voice low and gruff.

"Maybe you should teach me a lesson."

"Are you sure that's what you really want?" Liam asked. He moved a little closer so the bulk of his body was brushing against Felix's mostly bare skin.

"I've been spanked before."

Liam raised his eyebrows. "Oh?"

"In kink clubs."

"But you haven't had a Dom before?" Liam asked.

Felix shook his head.

"Then how do you know it's what you want?"

"I want you," Felix whispered.

"You barely know me."

"I know enough," Felix countered. "And I like everything I've seen so far." He curled his mouth into a naughty grin. "But maybe you're right. I think I need to see *more* of you." He swept his gaze from Liam's face, down his body, dying to see what was beneath the dressing gown and pyjama bottoms. "I need to see *all* of you."

"Do you?" Liam asked. It was the softest his voice had ever been.

"Most definitely."

Liam leant down, and for a dizzying second, Felix thought the man was going to kiss him. He wanted to be kissed so badly, but then Liam cleared his throat and stepped backwards. Air rushed between them, and Felix suddenly felt cold and exposed. He kept his arms by his sides, even though he wanted to hug them around his body.

"First, we need to talk. Then, and *only* then, we need to set some ground rules," Liam said sternly.

"Okay." Anything, so long as he got to feel Liam's touch. His body ached so badly, and he felt wound up like a tightly coiled spring.

"You can't rush into being someone's sub, Felix."

Felix dipped his chin. It wasn't that Liam was telling him off—his voice had lost its stern edge completely—but the man had made him acutely aware that he had been happy to rush into something without thinking it through. That was the story of his life, though. See an awesome coffee table, buy it. Want to get spanked and ordered around by a hot guy, go for it.

"What else have you done in kink clubs?" Liam asked. "Aside from being spanked. What else do you enjoy?"

"I've been tied up before." That had been fun. "I'd like to do that again."

Liam nodded. "When you were spanked, was it just with the palm of someone's hands or with a toy of some kind?"

"Hand and a paddle." Felix did a little wriggle as he remembered how that had felt on his arse.

"And you enjoyed that?"

"Yes, but I preferred a hand." His cheeks flushed as he wondered if he'd said the right thing.

"Have you tried anything else?"

"No… But I'm open to trying just about anything."

"Such as?"

Felix shrugged. "I don't know." When Liam didn't say anything, he thought about it a little longer. "There was one guy who was wearing a vibrating butt plug. His partner had the remote control. That was *hot*."

"You like the idea of using toys?"

Felix nodded eagerly.

"And of giving control to me?"

"*Yes*." Felix cleared his throat to try and get a hold of himself. "What do you like to do to your subs?"

"*With*," Liam corrected. "'To' implies a lack of consent."

"What do you like to do *with* your subs?"

"I like to spank them."

Felix beamed. "See, we're compatible."

Liam glowered at him, prompting Felix to shut up so the grumpy bear could continue.

"I like tying a boy up."

Felix shivered. "I'd try that."

"I like watching my boy."

Felix arched an eyebrow. "Watching?"

"As he comes."

"While you give him a blow job?" Felix ventured.

Liam shook his head. "From a distance, while he pleasures himself."

Felix inhaled sharply.

"Is *that* something you would enjoy?"

"Yes," Felix breathed. "I think I would."

"Is there anything you *wouldn't* do?"

"Not that I can think of, but if something comes up, I'll let you know."

"Good. You need to feel that you can talk to me, Felix. If you don't want to try something, or if you don't enjoy it when you do try it, you need to let me know."

"I will," Felix promised.

"Do you know about safe words?"

"Yes. They were used in the clubs I've been to. Everyone used the same ones."

"Which were?"

"Traffic lights. Red for stop, yellow for slow down, green for everything's fine."

"Are those good for you?"

Felix shrugged. "They're easy to remember."

"Good." Liam stroked his beard, making Felix want

to run his fingers through that thick auburn hair. "Then, if you still want me to be your Dom and teach you a lesson, we can talk about my rules."

Felix swallowed. "I do, so, so much." Their conversation had only made him crave Liam's firm hand even more.

"I'm serious about the rules I've already given you," Liam said. "And I have three more."

Felix waited, barely able to breathe.

"Rule number four. Your body belongs to me."

Felix nodded eagerly.

"Rule number five. Your orgasms belong to me."

Felix's eyes widened, and his breath caught in his throat. "Okay."

"Rule number six…" Liam paused, his lips parted, dragging the silence out to an excruciating length, that left Felix fidgeting with excitement. Liam folded his arms and stared into Felix's eyes intently. "I would like you to call me Daddy."

Liam's words caught Felix by surprise. "Daddy?"

"It better fits the type of Dom I am. I want to care for my boy and nurture him."

"I—" Felix wasn't sure what to say. "You're firm *and* caring?"

"Yes."

Felix stared at Liam, equal parts turned on and surprised.

"I can understand that you're surprised and that it might take you a while to get used to it. I also know that you might not feel comfortable calling me Daddy, and that would be okay too."

"It turns you on?"

"Yes." Liam's voice rumbled out from his chest, doing delicious things to Felix's body.

He felt his cock twitch and harden, which was impossible to hide in the tiny, skin-tight yoga pants. Not that Liam was looking anywhere but into Felix's eyes.

"If you want me to be, I'll be your Daddy, and you'll be my boy." He grasped Felix's chin in his hand, his grip strong but gentle. "If you're a good boy, I'll reward you, but if you're a bad boy, I'll punish you." He dropped his voice to a dangerous, growling tone for the last part.

Felix quivered, and his knees shook. Liam's grasp held him upright.

"I want you to be my boy, Felix. Do you want me to be your Daddy?"

9

LIAM

"Yes," Felix whimpered.

Liam resisted the urge to smile, taking another step back. The desperate look in Felix's eyes stabbed at his heart, but he'd already planned this moment, so he hardened himself to it.

"Take off those ridiculous things," he said, gesturing to the yoga pants.

He still thought they looked more like underwear than anything a sane person would exercise in. Despite that, they *had* caught his attention, and Felix *did* look stunning in them, especially now that his cock was straining against the stretchy fabric.

"Take them off?" Felix echoed.

"You heard me, boy," Liam snapped. "Don't keep me waiting."

Felix's hands went to his waistband, but then he paused. "But we're outside," he whispered.

"You have a high fence." Liam hadn't thought his

order would have been a problem for Felix. The boy was obviously somewhat of an exhibitionist. "I'm waiting," he repeated in an annoyed tone.

Felix gulped but obeyed, slowly pushing the yoga shorts over his hips, down his thighs, past his knees, to his ankles.

"Give them to me."

Clutching the shorts in his hands, Felix went to move closer. Liam put his hand up, forcing Felix to stop. He held his hand out, making sure their skin didn't connect as Felix handed the shorts over.

"Don't move," he said.

Felix clenched his fists, tapping them against his thighs as he glanced around. It was obvious he was looking at the fences that bordered his garden, specifically the back fence and the side that didn't connect to Liam's house. The border fences were too high for anyone to casually look over them, and walkers seldom went past, but Felix probably hadn't noticed that yet.

Liam pressed the shorts to his nose and mouth, inhaling. That snapped Felix's attention back to him. The boy stared at Liam with wide eyes. Liam took his time as he breathed in Felix's scent. He knew Felix wanted to be just as close to him; Liam wanted it to but not yet.

"Kneel."

Felix's knees buckled, and he dropped to the ground. He was so beautiful like that: naked, aroused, his face upturned, his neck craning so he could still look Liam in the eyes.

"Stroke your cock."

Felix's eyebrows knotted together, and again he hesitated. Clearly the boy's experiences in fetish clubs hadn't fully prepared him for being an obedient sub. Not that Liam had really expected them to. Every relationship between a Daddy and a boy was unique. Felix had indicated he was open to pleasuring himself while Liam watched, but Liam paused, allowing the boy time to think about what he was being asked to do, time to use the safe words they'd agreed on if he wanted to. Felix stayed quiet, his stare trained on Liam.

"Stroke your cock," Liam repeated, pushing annoyance into his voice.

Felix did as he was told, stroking his cock with a dry hand.

"Use your pre-cum," Liam instructed him.

Felix swiped at his slit with his thumb. There wasn't much of the thick, milky liquid there, but it was enough to slick his cock, which would make the hand job more pleasurable.

"Make yourself come," he ordered Felix.

"But—"

Liam narrowed his eyes, and Felix clamped his teeth together. Something flitted through the boy's eyes. Defiance, perhaps?

Felix inhaled deeply. "I want your hand on my cock. Or your mouth. I'm not fussy. I just need *you*."

"No," Liam said flatly.

Felix shrank back a little, his expression wounded.

"You're going to make yourself come," Liam told him. "Because I want you to."

Felix nodded and resumed stroking himself. It didn't take long for the unhappiness in his face to morph into pleasure. He lent his head farther back and worked his hand faster, groaning and panting. Like that, Felix reminded Liam of the painting. The boy was so beautiful to watch. The expression on his face was pure perfection. His muscles were relaxed, his eyelids loosely closed, his lips parted and wet, from where he kept swiping his tongue over them. A red flush had crept across his chest and shoulders. It was tempting for Liam to drop to his knees and offer to finish him off with his hand or his mouth. His own cock was hard but was hidden from view by the volume of his dressing gown.

As Felix hit his climax, a small cry tore out of his throat. His body shook over and over, and cum spurted from his cock in thick coils that spilt over his hand and dripped onto the freshly cut grass. Felix flopped his head forward, his chin resting against his chest as he breathed heavily. His body still trembled.

"Look at me." Liam made his voice a little gentler than it had been.

It took Felix a moment to comply, probably because he was summoning up the energy.

"You looked beautiful, boy, coming for me like that."

A fragile smile made Felix's chin quiver. "Was I good, Daddy? Did I please you?"

Liam hadn't expected Felix to call him Daddy so quickly or for it to sound so natural. He fought to retain his composure as his cock jerked and leaked pre-cum, making his pants warm and damp. He hadn't been called Daddy in far too long, and hearing it from Felix was close to perfect.

"Yes, boy," he said approvingly. "You were good, and you made me very happy."

Felix's tired smile became a little wider. "Do I get a reward? You said that—"

"I know what I said," Liam barked, cutting him off. "Yes," he spoke more softly this time. "You've earned a reward."

He closed the distance between them, bent down, and kissed Felix. The boy's lips tasted like roses bathed in sunshine, sweet and warm. Liam sucked Felix's bottom lip into his mouth, tasting him more fully. He nipped playfully at it and then demanded access to Felix's mouth with his tongue. His insides exploded with heat as he explored Felix's hot, needy mouth. He pulled away slowly, giving Felix plenty of time to accept the fact that the kiss was ending. The boy's skin was a little red from where Liam's beard had brushed against it, but the rash was already fading.

"Go inside," Liam instructed. "Clean yourself up and then have some breakfast."

"But—"

Liam gave him a stern look.

"Okay, Daddy," Felix said. "I'll do as you've asked. It's just that…" He stared at the ground.

"Patience, boy," Liam told him. "It will be worth the wait."

Felix looked up, his expression brighter.

"I'll look after you," Liam assured him.

"Thank you, Daddy."

Felix stood and practically skipped inside. Liam pressed the yoga shorts to his face, inhaling once more before heading back to his own house. He had an aching cock to deal with, and the image of Felix, naked and orgasming, firmly burnt into his mind to help him.

10

FELIX

Felix hadn't realised it was possible to be sated *and* frustrated at the same time. He obediently took a shower, too tired to be naughty by refusing to follow Liam's commands. While he stood under the warm water, he worked his mind over what had happened between them. It felt like very little, but also everything, and he had more questions than answers. Were they a couple now, or was this purely about sex? Not that they'd had sex. Even though Liam had barely touched him, the encounter had felt so intimate. Despite the physical distance between them, Felix had felt the heat rising from Liam's body. It had been intoxicating, but that feeling was fading now, washed away by time and water.

The orgasm had been great—better than he'd ever brought on using nothing but his hand—but the kiss had been otherworldly. It had felt like he was being kissed for the first time all over again. He didn't know whether it was because he was euphoric from the orgasm or wound up so tight by sexual frustration, but everything about it had been amazing, even the prickle of Liam's long, thick beard against his skin. The kiss had been tender and demanding, and he knew Liam had been claiming him, proving that he was in charge in that minute and every moment that was to come. The itchy rawness that he'd felt afterwards had gone, and he knew that, by the time he left the shower, there would be no evidence of the kiss on his face anymore. It was probably weird to ask for a more severe beard rash so he had something concrete to remember the kiss by, but he did all the same.

His limbs were still heavy when he dragged himself out of the shower and dried and dressed. He was supposed to get breakfast next, which gave him a moment's pause. How had Liam known he hadn't eaten yet, or had he just assumed that Felix had prioritised being an enticing tease over taking care of himself?

He was halfway through breakfast when the doorbell rang. He scooped up his bowl of cereal and went to open the door, still at least partially dazed from his early-morning antics. A man in casual but worn clothes stood on his doorstep. Felix blinked, not able to get his mind to tell him who it might be.

"I'm Spencer," the man said. "You asked me to come and quote for some decorating." Spencer checked his phone. "Have I got the right place? You're Mr Lee?"

Felix nodded. Spencer. He was the man who Liam had recommended.

"Wait—" Spencer said. "Are you?" He shook his head. "No, you can't be."

Felix half expected Spencer to rub at his eyes in disbelief, but instead, the man just kept staring at him

"You're the spitting image of Felix Lee," he said. "He's my daughter's favourite actor." He leant a little closer. "For these five minutes, anyway," he added conspiratorially. "I'm sure she'll have moved on to another hot young thing by next week."

Felix smiled and laughed.

Spencer squinted at him. "*Are* you?" He shook his head again.

"I'm Felix Lee," Felix replied, putting the man out of his misery. "Would your daughter like an autograph?"

Spencer gaped at him. "Are you for real?"

"Yes."

"Honest to God? You're Felix Lee?"

"Yes!"

"Well, bloody hell." Spencer rubbed the back of his neck. "I'll be damned. I've never met a movie star before. My daughter's going to scream the house down when she finds out. Would you really give her an autograph?"

Felix stood aside, giving Spencer room to step inside. "Why don't you do what you need to do to give me a quote, and I'll sort out the autograph for you?"

"What do you want done?" Spencer asked.

"The whole house is pretty dated," Felix said. "So I think every room needs freshening up." He smiled sheepishly. "But I don't really know what I want done yet. Maybe white, so it's neutral and bright? I'm planning on getting the bathroom and kitchen redone, so ignore those rooms for now, but quote me for everything else."

"Will do," Spencer said. He pulled a pad of paper, a pen, and some kind of gadget out of one of the pockets in his work trousers.

Felix left him to it, continuing to eat cereal as he wandered up to the spare room. He was pretty sure there was a box with photos that Emma had sent him for signing for fans. He wondered what Liam would have to say about him eating while he walked. He'd probably get told off. A ripple of excitement trailed down his spine, making him realise he was as excited about being punished as he was about receiving rewards. Of course, Liam might not care how he ate. He'd promised to take care of Felix, but that probably only meant sexually and not in his everyday life. Shame.

He set the cereal bowl aside to rummage through boxes, eventually finding a stack of photos of himself and a couple of silver Sharpie pens. By the time he was back downstairs, juggling the picture, Sharpie, and cereal bowl in his hands, Spencer seemed to have finished. His cheeks were an embarrassed shade of red. The painting. Felix hadn't even thought to cover it up for Spencer's benefit.

"I'll get this quote written up for you and dropped round in a day or two," he said. "If you want to go ahead, the lads and I can start in a couple of weeks. Is that okay for you?"

"More than," Felix said.

He hadn't expected anyone to be able to start straight away. Besides, having tradesmen in his house would be disruptive, although that would mean he'd have an excuse to invite himself over to Liam's more.

He put the cereal bowl down on the nearest surface, which meant ducking into the lounge to place it on the coffee table. That was another job he needed to do—get the tank in the coffee table set up and ready for fish.

"What's your daughter's name?" he asked.

"Natalie," Spencer said. "I still can't believe you're actually Felix Lee."

Felix held the photo up beside his face. "Definitely me."

Using the hallway wall for support, he wrote on the photo, being careful to use the negative space rather than writing directly over himself. When he was done, he waved the photo in the air a few times, encouraging the silver ink to dry before handing it over.

"Bloody hell," Spencer breathed. "Just you wait until I tell the lads that we might be doing a job for a film star. They're going to be gobsmacked."

Felix chuckled. Even if the girls he'd encountered on his walk hadn't already mentioned him all over social media, it wasn't going to be long before everyone knew he was living in the area.

He saw Spencer out, retrieved the cereal bowl, and took it into the garden to finish it. Domino raced out with him, sniffing around the garden as though it was the first time he'd been in it. The puppy began to investigate the grass where Felix had knelt at Liam's command. His cheeks coloured as he realised what it was Domino was smelling. As he jumped to his feet, the spoon fell from the bowl and clattered to the floor.

Ignoring it, Felix strode over to Domino, waving the puppy away from the remnants of his orgasm. The puppy wandered off and found a butterfly to chase, giving Felix the time to get a bowl of water to wash the cum away.

"What are you doing?"

For once, Felix hadn't even been aware that Liam was watching him; he'd been too focused on his task.

He grinned up at Liam, who was peering over the adjoining fence. "Clearing up." He nodded to Domino, who was down the far end of the garden. "He was a bit too curious."

Liam scowled. Was he annoyed at the dog or at Felix for washing away the evidence of their encounter?

Felix tossed the plastic jug onto the small patio and then went over to the fence. "I really enjoyed what we did earlier," he said huskily. "But I still really want to touch you. I want you to touch me."

Liam narrowed his eyes. "You're needy."

Felix laughed. "Is that a bad thing?"

Liam didn't answer.

"*I* don't think it's a bad thing," Felix stated.

Liam's hand was resting on the top of the fence, so Felix brushed his fingers over the larger man's knuckles.

"I want to see you naked," he whispered. "Please, Daddy?"

He could practically see Liam melting at the sound of the word 'Daddy', although he tried to hide it via a carefully schooled expression, which was bordering on angry. Felix didn't think that Liam really was angry; it was simply a silent way to tell him he was overstepping, that it wasn't *his* place to make demands.

"*Please?*"

Liam rolled his eyes. "So needy," he muttered grumpily as he pulled his hand away from Felix's touch and walked away from the fence, towards the greenhouse.

Felix's shoulders slumped, and he kicked at the grass.

"Are you just going to stand there?" Liam snapped.

He'd stopped halfway down his garden. His arms were folded, making the muscles in his arms bulge almost menacingly.

"Ummm..." Felix wasn't quite sure where Liam wanted him to go.

Liam pointed to the greenhouse. "I'll show you my plants *if* you hurry up."

"That had better be a euphemism," Felix muttered under his breath. "Coming, Daddy," he said in a louder, brighter voice.

He rounded up Domino and popped him inside the house, making sure he had plenty of water, and then hotfooted it out of his garden and into Liam's.

Liam was waiting for him in the greenhouse. Annoyingly, he was still fully dressed. Felix did have to concede that Liam looked pretty damn hot in the indigo jeans that clung to his tree trunk legs and showed off his arse and the bulge of his cock. If that was anything to go by, Felix wasn't going to be disappointed when he eventually got to see it. As usual, Liam was wearing a tank top. This one was grey and fairly close-fitting, accentuating the muscly bulk of his body. More than ever, Felix wanted to feel Liam's body against his. Given that the bear of a man was busy spraying the small potted plants, he doubted it was going to happen anytime soon.

"They're nice," Felix said a little lamely. "You really love gardening, don't you?"

"Yes."

"Did you get into it after you retired?"

Liam nodded. "That's when I moved here. I didn't have the time before."

"Why roses?" Felix asked.

Liam sighed. "It's hard to find beauty in the world when you're surrounded by the worst society has to offer. But even when I saw the world at its darkest, roses always seemed beautiful to me."

"Even though they have thorns?"

Liam shrugged. "Even the most beautiful things have their downsides." He glared at Felix. "Like you."

Felix pressed a finger to his chest. "Me?"

"You're beautiful but needy, and naughty."

"I think you like both of those things really," Felix teased. "You just don't want to admit it."

Liam put his hands on his hips and glowered at Felix. Grinning, Felix sauntered up to him and laid his hand on Liam's forearm, feeling his muscles. They were like iron, strong and unyielding.

"It took you long enough to admit you like me," he reminded Liam.

"I don't recall admitting that I like you," Liam replied indignantly.

Felix wrinkled his nose. "You just want to fuck me, then?" Even though his words were light, he felt a tug of disappointment in his gut.

There had to have been some kind of badge of honour for screwing a film star. God knew enough guys had earned it. He had let them. He enjoyed sex, but increasingly meaningless flings had left him feeling a little hollow. For some reason, he'd thought—hoped—that things might be different this time. Why set rules and ask to be called Daddy if this dalliance was going to be nothing but sex?

"Is that what you think?" Liam asked, his expression stern. "That all I want is to fuck you?"

Felix tried to make his shrug nonchalant. "It sure feels that way." He tilted his face up so he could stare into Liam's eyes. "Am I wrong?"

"You're the one who was demanding to see my cock." He brushed Felix's hand away from his arm. "You're the one who mentioned sex just now."

Felix forced himself to laugh. "Says the man who told me to strip and pleasure myself." He tried to sound flippant, but guilt crept into his voice. Liam was right. He had been the provocative one, the demanding one, the sexually needy one. "I'm sorry," he whispered, hanging his head. "I don't just want sex."

Liam put two fingers under Felix's chin and gently forced him to look up. "What *do* you want?"

"To be looked after… By *you*, Daddy." Felix was alarmed at the fragile tremble in his voice.

Liam let him go and nodded. "Then trust me to give you what you need, when you need it." He turned back to the plants. "Did you have breakfast?"

"Yes, Daddy."

Felix watched as Liam carried on spritzing the flowers. He wasn't sure if he was supposed to stay or go. Talk or stay silent. He'd never felt so out of his depth with a man while simultaneously craving him.

"What do you find beautiful, boy?" Liam asked.

"You," Felix said without hesitation. "You're amazing."

"What are my thorns?" Liam asked. "My downsides?"

Felix thought for a moment. "I find it hard to read you."

Liam glanced over his shoulder. "I thought you would say it was my grumpiness."

"No." Felix smiled softly. "I like that you're a grumpy bear."

Liam's eyes narrowed.

"But you *are* a grumpy bear," Felix insisted.

"Rule number one?"

"Don't wind you up," Felix said petulantly. "I won't do it again, grumpy bear."

"You're infuriating," Liam said in a warning tone. "Are you trying to annoy me?"

"Maybe," Felix admitted. "A little. Is it working?"

Liam growled deep within his throat.

"What would happen if I called you grumpy bear again?" Felix asked. "Theoretically speaking."

"I'd have to punish you," Liam said in a severe tone. "Is that what you want?"

Felix looked up and to the side, scrunching his lips up thoughtfully. "I'm not sure I can help myself. I am a very naughty boy." He shifted his stare back to Liam. "No one has ever given me real boundaries before. I was given curfews and things, but nothing happened if I broke them. Not even a slap on the wrists."

"Your chaperones didn't enforce discipline?"

"Not at all. Do you think that's why I'm so naughty?"

"Yes."

Felix sighed. "I'm not sure you *can* teach me how to behave, grumpy bear," he said melodramatically. "Maybe I'm a lost cause."

"Maybe." Liam scratched his chin through his beard. "Or maybe you just *want* to be punished."

He walked behind Felix, patting his arse before resting his hand over it. Heat flooded to Felix's groin, and his eyes flickered shut. It was hard not to press his arse back against Liam's hand. Somehow, he managed to hold himself still, simply savouring the way Liam's hand cupped his arse cheek.

"Do you like being spanked, boy?"

Felix shivered. "Yes."

"Do you want me to spank you?"

"More than anything."

Liam moved his hand and stepped in front of Felix,

arching an eyebrow. "More than you want to see my cock?"

Felix's cheeks blazed with heat, and he laughed. "Maybe not *that* much." He hitched in a breath. "Are you offering to show me your cock?"

"No," Liam said. "Not yet."

Felix pouted. "You're mean, grumpy bear."

Liam growled his displeasure at the nickname again, the sound louder and deeper than before. Felix sucked his bottom lip in, the anticipation killing him. Why was Liam allowed to tease and frustrate him so badly?

"I really want to see your cock, grumpy bear," he said, stamping his foot like a spoilt child for good measure.

"You're a brat," Liam snarled, although there was a hint of amused approval in his tone.

A brat? Felix could be a brat. He folded his arms and lifted his chin. "I want to see your cock," he demanded. "And you're a mean grumpy bear for not showing it to me."

He reached out to undo the button of Liam's jeans, but the older man reacted faster, knocking his hand away. Liam took hold of Felix's wrist and twisted it behind his back. It didn't hurt unless Felix tried to move. He stood still, breathing hard.

Liam's hot breath blew across his ear. "You're a naughty boy," Liam hissed. "And naughty boys need to be punished."

11

LIAM

Liam had enjoyed the build-up to this moment. He waited a couple of beats, giving Felix a chance to recant his taunts and apologise or even use his safe words. All Felix did was stand still, breathing hard and trembling slightly.

Liam let him go.

"I want your jeans and underwear around your knees so I can spank you," Liam ordered. "Now."

Felix obeyed without hesitation, proving to Liam that he had wanted to be punished.

"Lean against the table," Liam barked. "Arse out."

Felix did as he was told but added a sassy wiggle of his hips as he thrust his arse out. Liam sucked in a breath as quietly as he could, and his cock jerked in his pants. He wanted to free it and shove it inside Felix's arse, but it wasn't the right time for that yet, no matter how much they both wanted it.

He moved closer, stroking his hand over Felix's soft, tanned flesh. He loved the way Felix shuddered and moaned in response to his touch. Felix had been spanked before and would know what to expect, so Liam had no intention of going easy on him. If Felix wanted him to slow down or stop, he had their safe words.

Liam lifted his hand away, holding it high in the air. He waited, allowing Felix's anticipation to grow, watching the muscles in Felix's arse tense and relax over and over. Eventually, Felix waggled his arse again.

"I'm waiting, grumpy bear," he said.

Liam brought his hand down hard. The smack rang through the air. Felix hissed in a breath and cursed but stuck his arse out farther. There was a bright red handprint on his flesh. Liam smoothed his palm over the imprint, feeling the heat that he had caused.

He smacked Felix again, on the other side, harder than before. Felix's body shook, and he let out a cry that expressed pain and pleasure in a delicious sound.

"You're so naughty," he told Felix before smacking him again. "Calling me names." Another smack, even harder this time.

The next smack was the hardest yet. Felix sucked in a sob and lowered his head but didn't utter any safe words. His arse was fiery red and hot to the touch.

"Are you sorry?" Liam asked, giving Felix a chance to apologise and end his punishment.

Felix looked over his shoulder. His face was pale, and his forehead was beaded with sweat, but his grin was impish.

"But you *are* a grumpy bear, Daddy."

Liam spanked him again and again, spurred on by the sexy string of noises coming out of Felix's mouth.

"*Now* are you sorry?" he demanded. "Or does Daddy need to punish you more?"

"More, Daddy," Felix begged. "I haven't learnt my lesson yet."

Liam debated not giving Felix what he wanted, but he was enjoying himself too much to want to stop. He spanked Felix a few more times, switching arse cheeks every time one got too red to give it a small respite. When he saw Felix's arms shudder and almost buckle, he paused.

"I'm sorry, Daddy," Felix whimpered.

"For what?" Liam asked, gently stroking Felix's arse.

"For calling you names."

"Turn around," Liam told him, his voice commanding but soft.

Felix stood tall, visibly shaking as he turned around.

Liam opened his arms wide. "Come here, boy."

Felix shuffled forward until he was huddled up against Liam's chest. Liam held him as he began to cry.

"It's okay, boy," he whispered. "Daddy knows you're sorry."

He kneaded Felix's shoulders with one hand and stroked his still hot arse gently with the other. He could feel the boy's erection pressed against him and the dampness of pre-cum soak through his jeans to his skin, pleasantly warm. He could only imagine how frustrated Felix was feeling, how desperate he was for release.

Even though Felix was still sobbing, Liam pushed

him away. The boy swiped at his eyes, gulping air in an obvious attempt to get his tears under control.

"Do you want Daddy to take care of you?" Liam asked.

Felix nodded, his chin trembling.

Liam got down on his knees. He cupped Felix's arse cheeks in his hands, partly to steady the boy and partly to continue to stroke the sting away. He licked his tongue over Felix's slit, gazing up into his boy's heavy-lidded eyes as he tasted his pre-cum.

"You taste sweet," he said approvingly. "Just like you smell."

Felix smiled wearily.

"I rubbed your yoga shorts over my face while I pleasured myself," he told Felix. "I inhaled your scent as I came."

Felix's body shook. "Daddy..." He swiped his tongue over his lips. "Daddy, please." His voice was desperate.

"Needy boy."

"Yes," Felix whimpered. "I'm so needy for you. Please take care of me. *Please.*"

"Good boys don't ask," Liam reprimanded, stopping the soothing motions of his hands on Felix's arse and pulling his face back, away from the boy's cock.

Felix let out a pitiful whine. "I'm sorry, Daddy. I don't know how to behave. No one's ever taught me how. Teach me, Daddy. Tell me what to do."

"You'll stand there and take what I choose to give you," Liam said. "And you'll be grateful."

"Yes, Daddy."

"Run your hands through my hair," Liam commanded.

Felix did so, his touch gentle and rhythmic.

"Good boy," Liam said approvingly. "I like that."

He brushed his fingers up the shaft of Felix's cock, his touch whisper-soft. Felix groaned, and his eyes fluttered shut. His back arched, and his hips thrust forward, bringing his cock closer to Liam's lips.

Liam tutted. "Naughty boy."

A single sobbed escaped Felix's lips. "What did I do wrong, Daddy?"

"You moved," Liam said. "You were demanding."

"I didn't mean to be, Daddy. I couldn't help it."

"Well, now you know not to do it again, don't you?"

Felix nodded. Liam repeated the action. This time, Felix stayed completely still. More pre-cum beaded at his slit, so Liam pressed his thumb to the boy's frenulum and his forefinger to the other side of his cocktip, squeezing gently to milk as much pre-cum as he could. He smeared it over the head of Felix's cock, making it shiny and slick.

"Do you like that?" he asked, glancing up at Felix's face.

"Yes, Daddy."

The boy's face was slack, his head tilted back, his lips wet and parted. He looked so beautiful Liam had to catch his breath before he could do anything else.

He curled his hand around Felix's shaft and stroked up and down, squeezing a little more tightly as Felix started to moan. With each upward stroke, Felix's fore-skin brushed over his frenulum, producing more pre-cum, which Liam used to lubricate his hand and his boy's rock-hard cock.

"You're so beautiful," he told Felix. "Tell me how much you want me."

Felix made a garbled sound, and his eyebrows twitched together.

"What's the matter?" Liam asked. "Can't you talk?"

Felix shook his head.

"Tell me how much you want me," Liam growled, holding his hand still at the base of Felix's cock.

"I want you," Felix managed to choke out. "I need you."

As Liam started moving his hand back and forth again, he put his lips around the head of Felix's cock, tasting him once more. He was delicious. He took Felix farther into his mouth and moved his hands from the boy's shaft to cup, squeeze, and roll his balls.

"Oh, Daddy," Felix croaked out as Liam applied suction and swished his tongue over the hard, pulsing shaft.

Liam pulled his mouth free of Felix's cock completely. He was amazed that, although Felix had been gently stroking his hair the whole time, the young man hadn't once tried to move Liam's head to encourage him to take him in more deeply.

"You're being a very good boy," he said.

"Thank you, Daddy."

"I'm going to swallow you right to the back of my throat," Liam told him, smiling as Felix's cock twitched. "And you're going to tell me how good a job I'm doing."

He didn't give Felix a chance to protest, before

doing what he'd promised. He sealed his lips around Felix's shaft, sucking him in until the head of the boy's cock struck the back of his throat. Liam knew from his own experiences of being sucked off that Felix's body would be on fire with sensations. With the head of his cock nestled so deeply inside Liam's mouth, he would be experiencing a heady mixture of suction and friction.

"That's amazing, Daddy," Felix managed. "You're so good at this."

Liam breathed through his nose as he worked his mouth back and forth, sucking, licking, and making sure Felix's cock hit the back of his throat every single time.

"I can't think straight, Daddy," Felix whimpered. "You're making me see stars."

Good, that was exactly what Liam wanted. He squeezed Felix's arse cheeks, then pinched and kneaded them as he worked Felix's cock at an almost frenzied pace.

"I'm gonna come, Daddy," Felix gasped.

Liam felt Felix's cock stiffen even more and then hot jets of cum hit his throat. He swallowed them down, sucking Felix dry before releasing him from his mouth. He licked his lips and then pulled Felix's shuddering body down into his arms. He pressed his lips to Felix's and pushed his tongue into the boy's mouth so he could taste his own sweet cum. Felix moaned and whimpered as he allowed Liam to pillage his mouth. It was only when Liam felt a sob against his mouth that he ended the kiss. He held Felix tight, kissing the top of his head over and over.

"It's okay, boy," he whispered. "Daddy's going to take care of you."

He stood, lifting Felix in his arms and, cradling him against his chest, carried him out of the greenhouse and into his home.

12

FELIX

Felix lay on his side on Liam's sofa, propped up on cushions with a cosy blanket draped over him. Liam had made him some warm milk and given him sweet cookies, which he drank and ate gratefully once the urge to cry had left him. He felt a little ridiculous, but at the same time, his heart swelled that Liam was looking after him. His tight jeans chaffed against his still sore arse, and he wished he could take them off, but Liam hadn't given him permission to do so and had, in fact, redressed him after carrying him into the house. As much as Felix had enjoyed his punishment, he wasn't ready to receive another, so he put up with the discomfort.

Liam sat in an armchair, reading something on his tablet.

"Why did a straight-laced detective get into BDSM?" Felix asked once he'd grown bored of the silence.

Liam looked up from the tablet screen, glowering to show his annoyance at being disturbed.

"Sorry, Daddy," Felix said, taking a nibble from his third cookie.

He felt a lot better than when Liam had first brought him into the house. Less shaky and brain-fogged.

Liam snorted and turned his attention back to his tablet. Felix finished his cookie and then snuggled against the cushions, closing his eyes.

"For release," Liam said, breaking the silence.

Felix blinked his eyes open. He had no idea if a second had passed since he'd closed his eyes or several minutes. The quality of light in the room was the same, so he guessed he hadn't fallen asleep for any length of time, if at all, but he couldn't be sure.

"My job was stressful. I worked long hours and was strung out more often than not. I needed a way to truly let go."

Felix could understand that. Well, he could sort of understand that. Acting was worlds apart from being a detective, but the long hours and needing a way to let go was the same.

Liam rested the tablet on his knee. "How are you feeling?"

"A little fuzzy still," Felix admitted. "Sore."

Liam's eyebrows tugged down.

"It's a nice sore," Felix said hurriedly. "You gave me exactly what I needed, Daddy. You took care of me." He grinned, happy to see Liam's concerned expression relax slightly.

"You've given me two orgasms today," he mused.

"One. You gave the other to yourself."

Felix giggled. "True." He stared at Liam thought-fully. "But you haven't."

"I have," Liam reminded him. "Smelling your yoga shorts." He shifted in the armchair. "Don't worry about me, boy. I'm perfectly satisfied."

"Oh." Felix didn't even try to hide his disappointment.

"What's wrong, boy?"

"I want to pleasure you," Felix said. "To say thank you."

"You have nothing to thank me for. I'm doing what a good Daddy should. I'm taking care of my boy."

Felix pouted but didn't push the issue. "Could we at least cuddle, Daddy?"

Liam stood, putting the tablet on the side table beside his armchair. Felix shuffled aside to let him sit down beside him. Then he cuddled up to the bigger man, marvelling at how solid Liam's body was now that he was aware enough to truly appreciate it. Liam stroked Felix's arm, his fingers trailing up and down slowly and softly. The moment was all kinds of perfect. Felix felt warm and safe. He felt cared for in a way he'd never before experienced. There hadn't been this level of aftercare in the kink clubs. There had been some, of course. Doms were expected to make sure the subs they played with were okay after a session, but the way Liam looked after him was a whole new experience for Felix. It made him wonder what other surprises the man had to offer.

The doorbell ringing made Felix jump. It was a shrill sound that seemed far too loud, breaking the comfortable silence they'd lapsed into.

"Are you expecting someone?" Felix asked.

Liam shook his head.

"Ignore it?" Felix suggested.

"No."

He patted Felix's shoulder, prompting him to move. Felix did so, reluctantly, pulling a cushion into his arms, even though it was a very poor substitute for the man he'd just been hugging. He heard a muffled exchange at the door, and then Liam came back, holding a thick brown package.

"It's for you."

Felix frowned.

"Obviously you weren't in, so the driver tried here."

Felix made room for Liam again, accepting the parcel from him. From the weight and size, he knew what it was.

"It's a script," he told Liam. "My agent sent it to me to see if I want to audition for it."

"Do you?"

Felix chuckled. "I don't know yet, but probably not. I told her I was taking a break, but she didn't really listen." He tossed the package onto the floor. "She thinks I need to think about auditioning now because filming won't start for a while."

"She might be right," Liam said gruffly as he went back to stroking Felix's arm.

Felix shrugged. "Maybe."

"What TV show is the script for?"

Felix laughed. "TV—" He shook his head. "You've not seen anything I've been in, have you?"

"No."

"I don't do TV. Only films."

Liam's eyes widened, but he got his expression under control a second later.

"TV has the potential to be a much bigger commitment," Felix explained. "Especially in the US, where a short season will be eleven episodes, and a normal season will be twice that. It might be lower budget than film, but it takes longer. And if the show takes off..." He whistled. "Months could turn into years."

Liam stiffened. "How many films have you been in?"

Felix counted them off on his fingers by title from the earliest to the latest, surprising himself when he reached the total. "Thirteen." He laughed. "Do you think it's unlucky to take a break after thirteen films?"

"Thirteen?" This time, Liam didn't try to school his look of surprise.

"A lot of them were bit parts," Felix said. "When I was younger, I did cute kid roles with only a few lines. It's only recently that I've started getting bigger parts, which is probably why Emma—"

"Emma?"

"My agent. It's probably why she doesn't want me to take a break right now. She doesn't want my name or my face to be forgotten."

He thought back to the two encounters he'd had in the few days since he'd moved in. Emma was probably unnecessarily worried, but he was one of her meal tickets and her biggest at that. His parents had suggested he move to a new agent several times, one more experienced with dealing with big stars, but he'd refused. He liked and trusted Emma. She'd been his agent since his first film role, and although she could be somewhat pushy, she had always looked out for him.

He stared up at Liam, whose expression had become dark and brooding. Felix suddenly felt cold, so he shivered and pushed closer to Liam.

"Is something wrong?"

"No. I just didn't realise you were famous."

"I'm not sure I'm 'famous'. I'm not an A-lister, if that's what you're worried about." He smiled and nuzzled his cheek against Liam's chest. "More of a C-lister."

Liam relaxed a little.

"It's not a problem, is it?" Felix asked, worried.

"No."

Felix knew he shouldn't have expected anything more than a terse reply from Liam, but it didn't exactly set him at ease. What did help was the fact that Liam was still stroking him tenderly.

"I'm going to fall asleep if you keep doing that," he said sleepily. "Which means I like it. Keep stroking me like that."

"You'd better not fall asleep for too long. You've got a puppy to check on," Liam reminded him.

"Oh, shit." Felix hadn't meant to leave Domino for so long. "He'll probably have peed everywhere. You're right. I should go." He sat upright but instantly regretted it as the pressure on his tender arse made him bite his lip. He cupped his hand over Liam's cheek. "Come for dinner later? Around seven?"

"Not tonight," Liam said.

Felix frowned.

"Tomorrow."

Felix grinned happily. "Can I kiss you?" Felix wasn't sure why he was asking permission, but it felt like the right thing to do.

Liam fisted Felix's T-shirt and pulled him close into a hard kiss that left Felix breathless. His chin prickled from the texture of Liam's beard, but it didn't deter him from pushing into the kiss in an attempt to make it last as long as possible. Liam was a great kisser. Then again, Felix was beginning to think that Liam was great at everything: kissing, blow jobs... He quivered as his cock started to swell.

"I wish I didn't have to go."

"You need to take care of that puppy," Liam said sternly. "I'll see you tomorrow at seven."

Felix hoped he would see Liam earlier than that, in the garden tending to his roses, if nothing else. With that happy thought in his mind, he headed out of the sitting room.

"Boy." Liam's gruff voice halted him at the door. "Your script."

Felix's stomach sank a little, making him wish he'd been firmer with Emma when he'd told her he wasn't interested. Still, it was too late now. He would have to read it. He retrieved the still-sealed script, gave Liam a final cheerful grin, and left.

"Don't be disappointed," Felix said as he welcomed Liam into his house at seven the next evening. "I ordered takeaway."

Liam's face became cloudy.

"I can't cook," Felix said, embarrassed about it for the first time in his life.

"How have you survived?" Liam asked despairingly.

"On set, we're generally provided with food, and until I was eighteen, I always had a chaperone staying with me, so they cooked. Once I no longer needed one, I used takeaway, cereal, or ready meals to fill in the gaps."

Liam rolled his eyes. "You're twenty-five. You've had seven years to learn how to fend for yourself. It sounds like you've just been lazy."

Felix hung his head as he led Liam into the dining room, where he'd laid out the takeaway. He'd ordered Greek food this time and had made a pretty spread of the dishes he'd ordered. It smelt mouth-wateringly wonderful, and his stomach grumbled.

"I'll teach you to cook," Liam said, sitting down.

Felix sat opposite him. He leant his elbows on the table and rested his chin in his hands, curling his fingers over his jaw and cheeks. He batted his eyelashes. "Or you could just cook for me."

"Lazy," Liam huffed. "Just like I suspected."

"But you promised you'd take care of me."

"That doesn't mean I'm going to do everything for you, idle scamp. Have you ever put in a day's hard work in your life? Elbows off the table," Liam grunted. "You've no manners either."

"I'll have you know acting is very hard," Felix said indignantly.

He couldn't help but grin. This was the Liam he'd fallen for: gruff and finding fault with everything. He probably shouldn't have found it as sexy and endearing as he did.

"Lots of long hours on sets and location. Learning lines. And don't get me started on premieres," he added with a cheeky smile. "Meeting adoring fans is tiring." He yawned and stretched to emphasise his point. "It's no wonder I need a break."

Liam huffed out a breath. He looked utterly unimpressed.

"I hope you like Greek food," Felix said, serving them both a pork gyros wrap.

"I've never had it before."

"Then you're in for a treat."

"What's in it?"

"Spit roast pork, mixed salad, and tzatziki, smothered in strofilia dip and served in a pita bread."

"You sound like a menu. Did you memorise it?"

"I might have," Felix confessed. "It's nice. Give it a try."

He tucked in, watching Liam try the food more tentatively as he enjoyed his own. It was delicious. The pork was tender, and the salad was crisp. The tzatziki was a cool mix of yoghurt, cucumber, garlic, and mint, which was wonderfully refreshing. After his first few bites, Liam made a sound that could only be described as one of approval, bordering on pleasure. He ate more heartily after that.

They'd just finished the starter when Domino came bounding in. He had been asleep in the living room, but now he was wide awake and yapping to be played with.

Laughing, Felix stroked the puppy. "Later, Domino. We're eating."

The puppy sat down abruptly, staring up at Felix as he wagged his tail expectantly.

"This isn't your food," Felix told Domino gently.

He stood and patted his thigh, encouraging the puppy to follow him to the kitchen. He let Domino out into the garden to pee, while he put food out for him and then called him back inside.

By the time he'd washed his hands and returned to the dining room, Liam had dished up the main meal. Felix had ordered lemon chicken and a Greek salad, one of his favourite dishes.

"I rang the decorator you suggested," Felix said. "He should be giving me a quote in a day or two."

Liam nodded and glanced around. "It's very dated in here."

"I don't think it's been redecorated since the seventies," Felix agreed. "Although the surveyor said all the wiring had been updated five years ago, so that's something."

Liam looked at him with surprise.

Felix chuckled. "I'm not completely useless."

"What plans do you have?" Liam asked.

"I don't know what I want to do with the place, so I

asked him to quote for painting all the walls white. Boring, I know."

"Neutral," Liam corrected.

"It's definitely a blank canvas," Felix said. "I'll be able to go as outrageous as I want from there," he added in a teasing tone. "Do you think psychedelic walls would look good in here?" He widened his eyes in excitement. "I could get a mural of gorgeous nude men painted in my bedroom. Do you think it would be too much to put mirrors on the ceiling?"

"You're ridiculous," Liam said, glowering at his food.

"I could get the whole of the downstairs knocked through," Felix ploughed on. "To make it one huge party space. I've got to get some use out of that bar," he added, nodding towards the one in the corner.

It was made out of stainless steel, with a thick black strip, studded with crystals, about a quarter of the way down. What wasn't immediately obvious, because it wasn't turned on, was that there was also a pink lighting strip under the bar top.

Liam's expression became sour, as though he'd tasted something vile.

"I could get speakers built into the walls and loads of those Wi-Fi-controlled lights to create a disco effect."

"Rule number one," Liam growled.

"Don't wind you up," Felix said in a petulant tone. "But I enjoy it so much."

He knew he should back off because his arse was still tender from the spanking Liam had given him the day before, but teasing Liam was too much fun.

"Have you started to read the script yet?" Liam asked, putting an instant dampener on Felix's mood.

"No." He shovelled a fork full of chicken and salad into his mouth, chewing the lovely food sulkily.

"You're putting it off?" Liam asked.

Felix waved his hand absently. "I'll get round to it. There's no rush." He smiled. "Anyone would think you want me to audition so you can get rid of me."

Liam snorted. "It would certainly be quieter."

"Aww, but who else would annoy you?"

"Hopefully no one."

"You love it, really—" Felix cut himself off, shuffling to adjust his weight on his sore arse.

Liam grumbled something under his breath, which was neither clear nor loud enough for Felix to hear.

"I'm going to get a new bathroom and kitchen fitted," Felix said. "And I was thinking about extending the patio so I can get a hot tub." He waggled his eyebrows. "Would you join me if I did get a hot tub?"

Liam glared at him.

"Naked skinny dipping in hot bubbly water," Felix said. "You can't say it's not tempting."

The tiniest of smiles tugged at Liam's lips.

"Can I show you around when we've finished eating?" Felix asked.

"Is there much to see?"

"Probably not." Felix chuckled. "I've not unpacked anything, but I'd like to show you the house anyway."

Liam narrowed his eyes and stared at Felix hard as if trying to deduce something.

"Okay, yes," Felix said, squirming under the intensity of Liam's glare. "I just want to show you my bedroom. I bet you always played the bad cop when you were interrogating suspects, didn't you?"

"Oh, for the love of God," Liam breathed. "You watch too much TV."

"Probably." Felix leant onto his hand again. "Can I show you my bedroom?"

"Elbows," Liam scolded. "You've got sex on the brain."

Felix held his hands up. "Hey, you're the one who mentioned sex. *I* didn't say anything about having sex. *I* was just innocently inviting you to look at my bedroom."

"Innocently." Liam snorted.

"But if *you're* suggesting having sex, I'm not going to complain."

Liam rolled his eyes. "You are insufferable."

"Which you love," Felix said.

Liam let out an exasperated sigh, prompting Felix to back off a little; at least until they'd finished eating, anyway.

They finished their meals, and then Liam helped Felix to clear the dishes.

"I need to get a dishwasher," Felix mused as Liam washed and he dried.

"There's only one of you," Liam pointed out. "You'd need a week's worth of dishes to fill one."

"That would be pretty gross."

"It would be disgusting," Liam muttered.

"I think you can get mini ones," Felix said. "Cute little things that sit on a worktop."

"Cute?" Liam shook his head. "Only *you* would call an electrical appliance 'cute'."

Once everything was washed and dried, Felix put the plates and cutlery away. He'd barely finished when Liam cupped his arse cheeks, squeezing lightly before rubbing tenderly.

"How does it feel?" Liam asked, brushing his beard against Felix's jaw and neck.

"Tender," Felix breathed. "But getting better."

"Good." Liam rubbed a little harder.

"If you keep doing that, I won't be able to wait until after I've shown you my bedroom," Felix told him. "I'll want you to fuck me right here."

"I'm not going to fuck you tonight."

Felix twisted round so he could face Liam and pout at him. "But—"

Liam placed a finger over Felix's lips. "Not tonight, boy," he said firmly. "You need to learn patience."

"Are you going to teach me how to be more patient?" Felix whispered.

"Yes." Liam moved his finger and kissed Felix gently. "You were going to show me your bedroom."

Felix nodded dumbly. Somehow, Liam's words had been sexy as hell, even though he'd taken sex off the menu.

"I guess this is the same floorplan as your house?" he asked as he led Liam upstairs.

"It's the mirror image, but otherwise, yes."

Felix pushed open the door to his room. It was a bit of a state. He had a wardrobe, but all his clean clothes were heaped in an open suitcase. Emma had packed his clothes, but he'd made a mess of them when he'd searched for things and hadn't bothered to fold and tidy them again. His bed, which wasn't made, took up most of the space, and the nude painting—his pride and joy—was propped against the wall. He had no clue how to go about hanging a picture that size.

"Your bed is ridiculous," Liam grumbled. "It's far too big."

"But it's comfy," Felix said, flopping onto it. He patted the mattress beside him. "Want to try it out?"

Liam knotted his eyebrows together into a disapproving glower.

"It's got a music system built in," Felix informed him, pointing to the speakers and then to the controls. "And a bookshelf."

"With no books."

Felix waved his hand. "I told you I haven't unpacked. I do have books. It's also got a side table built in, with a safe under it," Felix went on. *He* was proud of his bed, even if Liam hated it. "And a massage chair."

"A what?"

"Massage chair."

Felix grinned and moved from the bed to the curved lounge chair that formed the left-hand edge of the bed. It was just wide enough to be comfortable. He felt around until he found the controller, which was attached to the bed by a thick black wire, and turned the chair on. It made a whirring sound as the massage rollers started to move beneath the padded leather. It was on the lowest setting, so provided a gentle kneading sensation that ran down the length of his body. It was a little uncomfortable against his arse, but not so much that he needed to turn the chair off.

He lounged, enjoying the massage, one arm tucked under his head. "Do you want to try it?"

"No."

"Do you know what I enjoy doing?"

"No, but I suspect you're going to tell me."

"I like to lie here, being massaged, stroking myself off while I stare at my painting."

Liam didn't turn to look at the painting behind him. There was no need, Felix decided. The man had already had an eyeful of it on moving day.

"I'd like to watch you do that," Liam said in a low, quiet tone.

"First, you watch me pleasure myself in the garden. Now, you want to watch me do it in my bedroom. Maybe you should just put a hole through the wall so you can watch me whenever you want." Felix had been joking, but his breath caught in his throat at the intense look Liam was giving him.

"A camera would be better," Liam said matter-of-factly.

Felix laughed nervously. "You're not joking, are you?" He cleared his throat. "You're into voyeurism?"

"If it's consensual." Liam looked around the room.

Was he trying to work out the best place to put a camera? The thought thrilled Felix.

"But how would I know when you were watching?" he asked.

"If it was a webcam, you would need to turn the stream on." Liam pinned Felix with his lust-filled stare.

"You wouldn't know if I was watching, but by turning on the stream, you'd be letting me know it's okay to."

Felix moaned. His cock strained against his zipper.

"Is the thought of me watching you turning you on?" Liam asked.

Felix nodded, silently praying that Liam would order him to undo his jeans and pleasure himself.

"Even if I'm in my own house, watching you on a screen?"

Felix wasn't sure if he'd thrown all rational thought out the window, but lust and excitement made him nod his head eagerly.

"That would make me very happy," Liam crooned.

"I want to make you happy, Daddy," Felix said breathlessly.

"And you will, boy."

Liam knelt beside him. He stroked Felix's hair tenderly and then kissed him in the same manner, slowly and softly.

"I'm going to go now," he said as their lips parted.

"But—"

"Hush," Liam said. "Have patience."

Felix didn't want to be patient. He wanted Liam's hands all over him, and his all over Liam. He wanted Liam's hot mouth around his cock again or to have Liam's cock in *his* mouth. He wanted Liam to stare at him with lust and approval as he stroked himself off. Most of all, he wanted Liam's cock up his arse. But he wasn't going to get any of it that night, because Liam was a huge fucking tease.

"There should be a new rule," he muttered.

"Oh?" Liam asked.

"No teasing *me*."

Liam chuckled and kissed him again. "I make the rules," he told Felix. "And that's definitely not going to be one of them."

Felix whimpered.

"You've got your hand, your massage chair, and your painting. I'm sure you can satisfy yourself tonight," Liam said. "Goodnight, boy." He kissed Felix on the forehead. "I'll see you soon."

13

LIAM

Over the next few days, Liam and Felix settled into a routine that felt like a dance of sorts. Felix would wake Liam far too early with loud but peaceful music, and he would wander out into the garden to watch Felix's sexy brand of yoga. Apparently, the yoga shorts that Liam had yet to return were Felix's only pair, so the boy took to doing the gentle stretching exercises in his boxer shorts. Liam approved because it gave him quite a show when Felix was in certain poses. He always made it clear he was at the fence, either by clearing his throat or rapping his fingers on the wood.

They bantered over the fence, Felix as cheeky as the day he'd moved in, not pushing quite far enough to deserve another spanking. Liam was a little disappointed by that, but he knew his boy needed time to recover. *His* boy. They'd known each other for a handful of days, yet that was how Liam already thought of the young man. Felix was *his* boy, a ray of sunshine in a life that had been quietly dismal for some time. Liam hadn't realised how dismal until Felix had stormed into it.

In the late afternoons, when Liam went into the garden to water the roses, Felix would come to the fence to ask about them. On the second afternoon, Liam told Felix about one rose.

"This plant is called Jean," he said, cupping one of the large rose heads in his hand. The petals were pale yellow, with darker pink tips, while the foliage was a rich, dark green. "My mother's name."

"I hadn't pegged you as a mummy's boy," Felix teased.

"I planted it to remember her by," Liam replied stiffly. "After she died."

"Shit, I'm sorry."

Liam waved away Felix's apology. "You weren't to know." He'd expected Felix to tease him. It was the boy's nature after all. "My parents had me and my sister later in life. She died peacefully in her sleep." He moved away from the rose. "And yes, I had a good relationship with her, so I suppose you *could* call me a mummy's boy, *if* you wanted a spanking."

Felix's eyes sparkled, but instead of taking the bait, he pointed to a rose with soft purple petals. "What about this one?"

"Not today."

"But—"

"*Not* today."

The next afternoon, Felix had asked Liam to tell him about one rose, of Liam's choice. Though he hadn't openly praised Felix, Liam had been proud of him. The young man was used to getting what he wanted when he wanted it, which was something he needed training out of. He needed to understand the beauty of waiting.

Each evening, Liam had gone over to Felix's house with a box full of cooking ingredients and all the utensils, pots, and pans needed to cook the dish. He stood to one side, issuing instructions, while Felix cooked or, at least, attempted to. The boy was a disaster in the kitchen, especially when it came to knives. Liam taught him how to cut properly and safely by standing close behind him and putting his hands over Felix's, guiding and instructing him. Liam had been forced to keep himself under control while they'd been so close so that he didn't get an erection.

After food, they sat on Felix's ridiculous purple sofa or out in the garden on the bench if the weather was nice enough, talking.

At the end of the first night, the only physical contact Liam had allowed other than the knife-wielding lesson was a passionate kiss that had left the skin around Felix's mouth scrubbed pink.

On the second night, he'd made Felix a mug of warm milk, and then they'd gone up to Felix's room. It was late, so Liam had instructed Felix to undress, wash, and brush his teeth, and then had tucked him up in bed, gloriously naked. Liam had wanted to join him; making Felix wait was torture for him too.

By the time the third night was drawing to a close, it was clear that Felix was frustrated and possibly going out of his mind. He pushed his teasing further and further, so Liam eased his torment a little by having him lie naked on the ostentatious massage chair in his bedroom, stroking his cock until he came. It hadn't taken Felix long, proving just how needy he was.

"Are you going to keep teasing me?" Felix asked as he saw Liam out.

"Yes."

Felix moaned and leant close, his face upturned, clearly seeking a kiss. "You're so mean to me."

Liam cupped Felix's face in his hand and gently kissed him on the forehead. "You'll thank me eventually," he promised.

"The other night…" Felix trailed off, dropping his gaze to the floor.

"What about the other night?"

"You talked about a camera. About watching me…" Felix caught his breath. "I thought you were serious, but I guess you were joking."

Excited warmth stirred within Liam's groin. "You've been thinking about that?"

"Yes," Felix whispered as he looked up again. His dark eyes were wide, his pupils blown. "I like it when you watch me."

Liam had been waiting for Felix to bring up the subject again because it almost certainly meant he had grown comfortable with the suggestion.

"I haven't watched you that often, boy."

"Not pleasuring myself, no," Felix conceded. "But you watch me every morning."

"Yes."

"And I like it," Felix persisted. "It excites me."

Liam stroked his hand down Felix's cheek, onto his neck, and across his shoulder. "It turns you on." It wasn't a question.

"Yes."

"Has anyone ever watched you come before? Anyone that wasn't pleasuring or fucking you at the time?" he clarified. It was wrong of him to hope that no one else had because he had no right to be jealous of Felix's life before they'd met, but the feeling was there nonetheless.

Felix shook his head, and Liam felt a little lighter and a little happier that he was the one to show Felix how pleasurable it was to be watched.

"Not even in the fetish clubs you went to?"

"No." Felix pursed his lips. "I mean… there were lots of other people in the room, but I didn't come when those men spanked me."

That made Liam happy too. One day soon, he would have to make Felix come just from a spanking.

"Coming in front of a camera would be different to having me with you," Liam warned. "You might feel self-conscious. You might not be able to get as turned on without me present."

Felix laughed. "I'm an actor, Daddy. I'm used to performing for a camera. I'm pretty sure I'll cope."

Liam tugged his eyebrows up in amusement. "Is this when you tell me that you're a porn star?"

Felix's laugh turned into a hearty cackle. "I'm definitely *not* a porn star."

"I wouldn't want you to fake anything on camera," Liam said, making his voice stern.

"I wouldn't, I promise."

Liam nodded thoughtfully. "*Why* do you want to do this, boy?"

Felix blinked up at him. "To make you happy."

"But will it make *you* happy?"

Felix nodded eagerly, swallowing hard. "I think so." He sounded breathless. "Yes," he said more certainly.

Liam glanced down at the telltale mound in Felix's pants. The boy was turned on just thinking about it. Watching him on camera was going to be hot as hell.

"I'll get you a camera to use."

Felix frowned. "I have one built into my laptop."

Liam glowered at him. "Have you any idea how terrible the picture quality is on those things?"

Felix shrugged.

"It's awful," Liam barked. "I want to be able to see every inch of you clearly."

Felix sucked in a quivering breath. His forehead creased, and he adjusted his jeans. Liam could tell he needed release. He ached to give it to Felix. He could put him over his shoulder and carry him upstairs, strip him naked and fuck him until he came so hard he was delirious. He felt his cock twitch and immediately reined in his thoughts. Soon, he promised himself. He'd bury his cock in Felix soon.

He kissed Felix again, properly this time, wrapping the boy tightly in his arms as he nibbled his lip, sucked on his tongue, and made his face red again with his beard. Then he stepped back, putting cool distance between them and, as their dance ended for another night, said goodbye. He had a slight skip in his step as he walked back to his own house, excited by the thought of choosing and ordering a camera for Felix to use. Thrilled by the idea of giving his boy a new and pleasurable experience.

14

FELIX

—H*ave you read the script yet?*

Emma's daily text messages were starting to get annoying. Of course, it was Felix's fault for not reading the script. He could have made time, but between flirting with Liam, cooking lessons, attempting to train Domino, and dealing with tradesmen traipsing through his house to give him quotes, he hadn't.

He ignored the text and headed out into the garden, Domino chasing along at his heels. He grabbed a ball and played fetch with the puppy, laughing as Domino tripped over his feet more often than not in his hurry to get to the ball. Domino would grow into his paws eventually, but he wasn't there yet.

"Shouldn't you be reading that script?" Liam asked from the other side of the fence. "Not wasting time."

"Don't you start." Felix sighed. "My agent is already on my case."

Liam leant on the top of the fence. "Shouldn't that tell you something?"

Felix tossed the ball for Domino before wandering over. "Is this where you tell me how lazy I am?" He made sure the comment sounded flippantly cheeky.

"You are," Liam huffed.

"Well, you could invite me over and put me to work," Felix suggested. "I wouldn't be lazy if I was on my knees, with my mouth around your cock."

Liam rolled his eyes. "Lazy and single-minded. Is sex all you think about?"

There was a soft thud as Domino dropped the bright red ball at Felix's feet. He crouched down to retrieve it, stood, and threw it to the other end of the garden. The puppy raced off excitedly.

"I also think about you fucking me," Felix said with a shrug. He beamed up at Liam. "When *are* you going to fuck me?"

He would have loved to have had X-ray vision so he could see through the fence. That way he'd know if his flirtatious comments were getting a rise from Liam's cock. He hoped they were.

"It's hard to think about anything else when you've got me so frustrated," he pointed out. "I *need* you, Daddy," he whined.

Liam narrowed his eyes. "So you're telling me you can't read the script until I give you a good fucking?"

Felix rolled his eyes and pursed his lips, pretending to think. "Yup," he replied after a slight pause.

"Ridiculous," Liam said scathingly. "If you don't want to read it, just be honest with your agent."

Felix rubbed his jaw. "If only it were that simple."

"It is."

"It's not."

Domino chose that moment to return the ball.

"Are you answering back, boy?" Liam demanded.

Felix avoided answering by squatting to pick the ball up. He tossed it from hand to hand, much to Domino's annoyance. The puppy sat and whined, turning his head back and forth to watch the ball. Despite that, Domino's tail wagged across the grass. Felix knew how the puppy felt: frustrated at being at someone else's every whim but excited by it at the same time. He threw the ball, not as far this time, and then stood to face Liam.

"If I was answering back, would you punish me?"

"Not this time," Liam said sternly.

"Don't you want to spank me?"

"Yes," Liam said through gritted teeth. "But you're using naughtiness to avoid having a serious conversation."

"I am?"

"You know you are. The real question is why?"

"Why…?"

"Why don't you want to tell me why you can't just refuse to read the script? Why don't you want to read it in the first place?"

"That might be a few too many questions for my lazy brain to handle," Felix retorted.

"This isn't the time for childish games, boy."

Felix dropped his chin to his chest. "Sorry, Daddy."

"Why did you want to take a break in the first place?" Liam asked.

Felix debated pointing out that that wasn't one of the questions Liam had just asked, but he decided not to push his luck. "I've been acting for years. When I first started, I had big breaks between films, but the last few years I've gone from one film to the next. I've spent more time in trailers on location and in hotel rooms near studios than in the flat I was renting in LA. It's been nonstop, and I'm *tired*." He took a breath. "I love acting, but I was in serious danger of burning out. I need a time out before that happens."

"But you plan to go back?"

Felix hesitated. "Yes."

Liam's eyebrows punched together for the briefest of seconds. "You're sure?"

"Yes," Felix replied more confidently. "Emma thinks that all it will take is one big role to catapult me onto the A-list, which is why she's already on my case about finding that life-changing film."

"And you don't think you need to look just yet?"

"Maybe I'd just hoped I didn't need to." Felix sighed. "I guess I should trust Emma's judgement. I just thought I'd have more time before I started the auditioning again."

"Why can't you just refuse to read the script?" Liam asked. "And tell her to wait a month before she bothers you with one again?"

"Emma's been my agent for years," Felix explained. "She's worked really hard to get me where I am. It feels really ungrateful to throw this script back in her face."

"But she knows you want a break?"

Felix nodded. "But filming won't start on this project for a while. In *her* eyes, I'll get my break *and* I'll have a film lined up."

"That makes sense."

Liam ran his fingers back and forth over the rough fence. The stain probably needed refreshing, Felix noted, as he became mesmerised by the movement of Liam's fingers. Another job to add to his list, one he could easily do himself rather than hiring someone else. That would show Liam he wasn't bone idle.

"You don't think you'll be ready to go back to acting by the time filming starts?"

Felix shrugged. "I don't know. That's the problem."

"Is the part yours if you want it?"

Felix shook his head. "No. I'd have to audition, which would probably mean a trip to the States pretty soon. Sometimes they do local casting, but not this time."

"They want an American for the role?"

"Or someone who can pretend to be," Felix said, putting on a relaxed, Californian accent. "I can do New York and Chicago too. Do you want to hear?"

"No."

Felix pouted. "I'm good at dialects."

"I'm sure you are, but you're trying to distract me, and it won't work. Why don't you want to audition?"

Felix ran a hand through his hair, messing it up. "Auditioning is as good as committing to the film. *If* they like me, I wouldn't be able to back out without making a bad name for myself. Casting agents, directors, producers... *None* of them like being messed around. I'm nowhere near big enough to act like a diva."

Liam raised his eyebrows. "You *don't* act like a diva?"

Felix laughed. "Believe it or not, I'm always on my best behaviour when I'm on set."

Liam's face twisted into a sour expression. "I don't believe it."

"Ask my agent. She'll tell you how great I am to work with."

"So it's just me you're naughty for?"

"*Maybe*," Felix replied in a not-so-innocent tone.

He looked down as Domino rubbed against his leg. The dog had abandoned the ball and now just seemed to want attention. Smiling, he scooped the puppy into his arms and scratched his head.

"You're going to be too big for me to pick up soon," he told the puppy. "What will I do with you if I have to go to the States?"

"How long would you be gone for?"

"For the audition?"

Liam nodded.

"Not long. A few days at most."

Liam put his hands on his hips. He seemed to be deep in thought for a moment before he heaved out a great big sigh. "Leave him with me."

Felix gasped. "Are you serious?"

"Yes."

"I really want to hug you," Felix said. "You're the best." His happiness was short-lived. He slumped his shoulders and puffed his cheeks out, slowly exhaling. "If I get the part, I'd probably be gone for weeks or even months for filming." He scratched Domino behind the ears and looked at the house. "Seems weird to even think about leaving when I've only just moved in." He stared into Liam's eyes. "And I know we haven't known each other for long, but I'm not loving the thought of leaving you either."

Liam reached over the fence to ruffle Felix's hair. "You're worrying about something that might not happen. Is your agent expecting you to audition?"

"Only if I like the script."

"Then the first step is to read it and see if you love it," Liam said.

It felt like Felix was being given an instruction rather than a suggestion.

"*If* you love it, then the next step is to go to the audition. *If* you get the part, *then* you can work out what to do about your dog and everything else."

Felix hoped Liam was including himself in the catch-all phrase of 'everything else'.

"Read the script," Liam ordered. "Today."

Felix opened his mouth to argue but stopped when Liam twisted his hands into his hair. There was a small amount of pain, not so much that Felix wanted to yelp but enough to know that Liam meant business. The weird thing was, he felt safe. He knew he could say 'red' and Liam would stop.

"Yes, Daddy."

"Good boy." Liam loosened his grip on Felix's hair and ruffled it again affectionately. "I'll see you when you've finished."

"Wait... What?" Felix exclaimed. "I can't take a break and come suck your cock?"

"No," Liam growled. He let go of Felix's hair. "You

don't get to touch or be touched until you've read the whole script."

"And once I have?"

The corners of Liam's lips twitched up ever so slightly. "Then you can have a reward."

15

LIAM

With a small package tucked safely under his arm and a bag of tools slung over his shoulder, Liam knocked on Felix's door at eight. It was hard to maintain a neutral expression when a weary-looking Felix opened the door and instantly brightened up. His eyes sparkled in the evening light, and a grin spread across his lips.

"Have you finished?" Liam asked.

Felix slouched. "Not yet."

"Have you eaten?"

"Yes, which is why I haven't finished."

Liam nodded approvingly. At least his boy had taken care of himself.

"Are you here to give me a break?" Felix asked hopefully.

"No."

Felix pouted, which was absolutely adorable. It was difficult to resist pushing him inside so he could kiss the pout of the boy's face, but Liam managed to restrain himself.

"Why are you here?" Felix asked. His stare found the package under Liam's arm. "Is that a present? For me?" His voice quivered excitedly.

"Not exactly. Can I come in?"

Felix's lips turned up again. "Please do."

He moved aside but not far enough to allow Liam in without their bodies brushing in some manner.

Liam scowled at him. "What did I say earlier?"

"No touching or being touched until I'm done with the script." Felix gave Liam huge puppy dog eyes. "You're mean. I only want a kiss."

Liam knew a kiss wouldn't sate his boy. At this stage in their dance, it wouldn't sate *him* either. Felix reached out, so Liam stepped back.

"I *was* going to set something up while you finished reading the script, but if you're going to be naughty, I'll leave."

Felix tipped his head to the side, eyes narrowing as his stare homed in on the package tucked under Liam's arm again. "Set something up…" he echoed. His eyebrows shot up. "Is that a camera?" He shifted his weight from foot to foot excitedly.

Liam half expected Felix to clap his hands; it would have been sweet if he had done. "Yes."

Felix gasped. "Thank you!"

Liam was glad the boy was still excited about the concept of being watched remotely. It was important to him that Felix was not only accepting of the idea but that he wanted it too.

"Go back to your reading while I set this up," Liam ordered. "I'll need your laptop."

This time, Felix moved far enough away that Liam could enter the house without any danger of touching one another. Liam's body cried out for Felix, but he resisted. It was good that they were both feeling somewhat frustrated, as it would make the moment they had intercourse all the sweeter.

Once Liam was set up with everything he needed in Felix's bedroom, he sent the boy away. Felix still hadn't made any attempt to unpack. No doubt he was stalling until after the decorators had done their work, but Liam doubted that everything would get put away then either. He imagined that Felix was used to living out of suitcases when filming, based on what he'd said earlier.

He couldn't imagine moving around so much and not being able to put down roots. Even before Liam had bought his current house, he'd been a homebody. Despite the noise due to its location, he'd liked his flat in London. It had been his safe haven after long and stressful hours at work, a place where he could fully wind down.

He got the webcam set up with the laptop first, noting that Felix didn't have internet access in his home yet. Not that it mattered. There was no way Liam was going to risk the boy broadcasting sexy live streams over the open internet. Obviously, he didn't want anyone else to see them, but he also wanted to protect Felix. Even a C-lister's reputation and career could get badly damaged if that sort of video was leaked. With that in mind, he had always intended for them to use his secure network so that the live stream was only ever internal.

Once the camera feed was displaying on the laptop, Liam worked on finding the best place to put it and then he secured it to the wall. It didn't take long, so he doubted Felix would have finished reading the script.

After going downstairs, he stood in the doorway to the lounge, watching Felix. The boy was curled up on the sofa with the puppy. He was staring at the script intently while absently stroking Domino's head with his free hand. A half-empty bottle of water stood on the floor within easy reach, making Liam smile.

He cleared his throat. "I'm all done."

Felix jerked his head up. "That was fast." He smiled impishly. "Would you believe me if I said I was on the last page?"

It was obvious that Felix *wasn't* on the last page.

"No."

Felix sighed. "Shame. I was hoping we could test the camera out tonight."

The boy's grin was almost impossible to resist, but Liam couldn't give in. He'd told Felix he had to finish reading the script before anything else happened between them, and he was going to stick to that. He wouldn't be able to teach Felix discipline if he wavered every time the boy tried to bewitch him with his beautiful, sexy smile.

"Is it good?" Liam asked, nodding to the script.

"Yeah, it is." Felix sounded almost disappointed that he was enjoying it. "It's a good, solid story. The writing is great, the characters are interesting..." He sighed.

"You want to audition for it, don't you?" Liam asked. His gut twisted at the thought.

"I'll see how it ends," Felix replied. "Even the best films can turn to trash in the last few minutes." He started to flick through to the end.

"No peeking," Liam chastised.

Felix batted his eyelashes innocently. "It would save us both some frustration if I checked out the end," he pointed out. "If the ending's good, I'll audition. If it's not…" He shrugged. "I don't need to read every single word, do I?"

"Yes."

"But why?"

"You need to learn patience," Liam reminded him. "You wanted me to teach you how to behave. Right now, I'm teaching you not to cut corners."

Felix huffed out a breath. "Fine." His expression brightened. "But could you at least give me a kiss before you go? I have been a good boy so far after all."

Liam pinched his eyebrows together. "Not from where I'm standing, you haven't."

"Then give me a quick spanking for being naughty," Felix begged. "Just a couple of smacks."

"If you're that eager for a spanking, I might need to find some other way to punish you."

"One I'll like more?"

Liam almost laughed at that. Although it was good that Felix wasn't afraid of being punished, because it meant he would continue to be naughty. Liam definitely liked Felix's bratty side. Besides, he'd already seen plenty of proof that Felix *could* restrain himself when he was too sore to receive another spanking.

"You want to, don't you?" Felix asked.

"Want to what?"

Felix rolled his eyes. "Spank me before you go. You're tempted. I can see it in your eyes and…" He looked down instead of finishing his sentence.

Liam glowered at his boy, but he was really annoyed at his body for betraying him. It was hard to be the disciplinarian when his cock wouldn't behave. Felix deserved to be punished for pointing Liam's hard-on out, which was probably why the boy had drawn attention to it. He really was naughty.

"I do," Liam admitted. "But I'm not going to."

"Why?" Felix whined.

"Because you want it *too* much, and right now, denying you is a bigger punishment than spanking you. Goodnight."

He turned to go, but Felix's voice called him back.

"Grumpy bear…"

The urge to tip Felix over his lap went up tenfold, but Liam knew that had been the boy's intention.

"Goodnight, Felix," he said tersely. "Finish the script, and then we'll play."

Felix didn't wake Liam up with obnoxiously loud yoga music the next morning, which either meant he hadn't finished reading the script, or he'd stayed up late to do so and was sleeping in. Liam forced himself to go about his day as normal. Or at least his old normal, pre-Felix. Wake early—without his Felix-shaped alarm clock—do one hundred press-ups—he could really tell that he hadn't done them in several days—shower, and have breakfast. His muscles ached from the press-ups, not at all soothed by the shower. It was amazing how big an effect taking a few days off could have on his body. It was probably a sign he was getting old—*older*. No more slacking off, he decided. He'd either have to get out of bed before Felix or ignore the siren call of the yoga music each day.

Liam had been working in the garden for some time —weeding and pruning—before Felix finally appeared. Liam heard Domino first. The puppy burst into the garden, yapping loudly. The sound was piercing, making Liam wince and grumble under his breath. He stood tall, watching as Felix followed the puppy at a much slower pace. His hair was messy, and he was only wearing a pair of boxer shorts. Not that Liam was complaining. Felix stretched and yawned, giving Liam a sleepy wave as he approached the fence.

"Hey, neighbour," Felix said around a second yawn. "I finished reading the script last night."

"Is that why you've been lazing in bed all morning?"

Felix looked at his bare wrist and then chuckled. "I guess so. What time is it?"

Liam checked his own watch. "Gone eleven."

"Very precise." Felix yawned again.

"Was it good?" Liam asked. "Or did it have a rubbish ending?"

He realised he was hoping for the latter.

"It was great." Felix's voice held more enthusiasm than the night before, albeit tainted by a weary heaviness. "I've texted Emma to tell her I'll audition."

"When?" Liam asked, holding his breath.

Felix shrugged. "No idea." He put his hands on his hips and began stretching slowly from side to side. "She'll let me know the details when she has them."

"You'll need to book flights?"

"Nah, Emma deals with all the logistics."

Liam raised an eyebrow. "You've never had to do anything for yourself, have you?"

Felix grinned. "I have to make myself breakfast every day. That's hard work." He tilted his head. "I guess it's too late for breakfast. Although I could devour *you* if you let me." He licked his lips, making Liam want to vault over the fence to kiss him senseless.

"I can touch you now, right?" Felix asked hopefully. "*You* can touch *me*?"

"I want to watch you," Liam said.

Felix sucked in a breath. It was obvious he wanted to be watched. The question was, did he want to be watched or touched more? Liam waited patiently for Felix to speak, equally prepared for him to submit or answer back. Whichever tact Felix chose, Liam would enjoy himself.

"I want that too," Felix whispered, a blush creeping into his cheeks. "But I want you to touch me as well. I want..." He breathed in deeply. "I want you so badly, Daddy."

"I know," Liam said. "But I want you to be patient for a little longer. Can you do that, boy?"

Felix nodded uncertainly.

"Can I come round and finish setting things up?"

"Yes."

"No touching," Liam warned.

"No touching," Felix agreed, although there was definitely a hint of petulance in his voice.

It didn't take long for Liam to connect Felix to his network and show him how to turn the video on when he wanted to.

"It won't record anything on either end," he told Felix. "And you'll be streaming on an internal network with a heavy-duty password on it."

"Isn't that overkill?"

"I want you to feel completely comfortable and safe doing this. No one will see it but me, and there won't be a recording for me or anyone else to use at a later date."

"You're not talking about a personal rewatch to get off, are you?" Felix asked, nervousness making his voice wobble.

Liam fought back the urge to cup Felix's cheek in his hand. "No. You're in the public eye, Felix. It wouldn't be good if a recording of you pleasuring your-self got out onto the internet."

Felix shuddered. "Emma would have a fit."

"And how would you feel?"

"It would be awful." He looked up into Liam's eyes. "Thank you for protecting me."

Liam smiled softly. "I'm going to go home now."

"To watch me?" Felix asked eagerly.

"Yes."

"What do you want me to do?" Felix asked. "A hand

job or…?" He lifted his eyebrows. "I could finger myself for you, Daddy. Or I've got a dildo and I could—"

"No!" Liam snapped. "The only thing I want to see inside you is my cock."

"I wish you were offering to fuck me right now," Felix moaned.

"Soon," Liam promised.

"I know, I know, I have to be patient. I'm trying, Daddy, but it's *hard*." Felix chuckled. "Pun absolutely intended." He slid his hand down the front of his boxer shorts. "I'm already hard for you, Daddy. Do you want to see?"

Liam did, but he shook his head sternly. "I'm going home now," he repeated. "Start the stream whenever you're ready."

He strode to the door. "And, Felix…"

"Yes, Daddy?" Felix asked, eyes wide.

"It's okay if you're *not* ready. I won't be angry. This is a big step. It's something you haven't done before. I'll understand if you decide you don't want to do it yet or at all."

"I do," Felix insisted. "I want to make you happy."

Liam narrowed his eyes. "I'm glad you do, but I don't want you to do anything that makes you feel uncomfortable or weird. Do you understand?"

Felix nodded.

Liam couldn't help himself. He returned to Felix and kissed him swiftly. Their lips were barely connected long enough for their tongues to swipe against each other. Then he left before his resolve not to continue to make Felix wait crumbled completely.

16

FELIX

The first thing Felix did was take a shower to make sure he was clean inside and out. It might have been slightly wishful thinking, but he could hope. He didn't bother with boxer shorts. Instead he left the towel wrapped around his waist and sat on his bed, staring at the camera. His breath caught in his throat, and his body felt tingly. One second, he was grinning like an idiot; the next nerves were fluttering in his stomach. He would start to stand, to go and turn the stream on, and then stay firmly where he was. He hadn't been lying when he'd told Liam he wanted to do it, but now that the moment had come, it felt weirdly daunting. He was used to acting for a camera, and this shouldn't have felt any different, but it did.

He wasn't in a studio or on location with dozens of cast members and crew around him. There weren't several massive cameras or a director to tell him what to do. Even Liam hadn't given him any direction at all, except the order not to finger himself or use a dildo. The two times Liam had watched him, he'd told him what to do. It wasn't that he didn't know what to do—*obviously* he knew how to make himself come—but he didn't know what would please Liam, and that was more important to him than his own orgasm.

He pushed his hands into his hair and took a few deep breaths to centre himself.

Liam would already be in his room or wherever he was going to watch from. Felix was sure of it. He would be watching his computer screen—did he have a laptop or a desktop machine?—waiting. He might have changed into something more comfortable. Hell, he might have been sprawled naked on his bed, already stroking his cock while he waited.

A small moan tore from Felix's throat. He hadn't seen Liam's bedroom yet, and he had only been able to imagine what the man looked like naked. No one had ever made him wait like this before, nor had anyone been content to stand back and watch him while he reached climax, either in person or via a camera. They weren't in the same room, and yet the thought of turning on the stream felt more weirdly intimate than anything Felix had ever done before. With the way his head was whirling, butterflies whipped up a storm in his gut. Felix realised it would be a bigger commitment than sex. If he turned it on and pleasured himself, he would be stepping fully into Liam's kinky fantasy.

Was that why Liam had forced him to wait for sex?

He'd promised he wouldn't be angry if Felix didn't turn the stream on if he wasn't ready now or ever, but 'not angry' was not the same as 'not disappointed'. 'Not angry' wasn't a promise that they'd stay together, or that Liam would even want him if he couldn't. Voyeurism was something Liam enjoyed. Could he have a relationship with a man who didn't want to be watched? Were they in a relationship at all, or were they just neighbours with benefits? Felix thought he knew that answer to that, but it wasn't as if they'd had a conversation about it and defined what the hell it was they were doing. But if things weren't as serious as Felix thought, it would be easy for Liam to call time out on whatever it was they had.

He clenched his hair. He had to get those thoughts out of his mind. There had been no hint in Liam's voice, face, or kiss, that he would end things if Felix didn't turn the stream on. Those were Felix's insecurities talking. He was too used to short flings, to being used as a fashion accessory because his face was instantly recognisable. These past few days with Liam had been different. The man hadn't even known who he was, nor had he seemed even remotely star-struck when he'd found out. Liam wanted *him,* and by God, Felix wanted Liam too.

He blew out a breath and then looked around, trying to figure out a good place to lie to give Liam a good show. The massage chair was probably best, plus it would help to turn him on. The hard-on he'd developed when Liam had been in the room with him had gone. He'd need to wake his cock up again before he turned the stream on. Briefly, he debated being naughty and using his dildo. At the very least it would lead to a spanking, if not a fucking, but he didn't feel disobedient. All that mattered was making Liam happy, and he *really* wanted to make him happy.

He discarded the towel, got some lube, and settled down on the massage chair, turning it on. His gaze went to the painting as he started to stroke his flaccid cock. Normally, it would be standing to attention in seconds, but for once, the painting wasn't doing it for him. He hitched in a breath, briefly confused until he realised that it was a poor substitute for Liam's hulking, demanding presence. He bit his lip, wondering if turning the stream on and staring into the camera would help him. At least he'd know Liam would be watching, even though he wouldn't be able to see his Daddy.

His heart hammered as he stood and crossed over to the laptop on wobbly legs. This was it. If he turned the stream on and brought himself to climax in full view of the camera, there would be no going back. The butterflies swarmed from his stomach to lodge in his throat, and he felt momentarily dizzy. There would be no shame in backing out. Liam wouldn't think any less of him. But he didn't want to. As nervous as he was, he did want to do this for Liam. He wanted to share the next few moments with the man, even though they wouldn't be in the same room. He swallowed the butterflies away, took a deep breath, and turned the stream on.

17

LIAM

Liam had made himself comfortable while he waited for Felix to start the stream, all the time reminding himself that the boy might not turn it on at all. Flirtatious excitement might give way to nerves, or Felix might realise that it wasn't something he wanted to do at all. That would be fine. Liam hoped he'd made that clear.

He was about to give up and go back to Felix's house to tell him it was okay and to hug him tightly to prove it when the black picture on the laptop screen switched to a close-up of Felix's bare chest. The boy ducked so his face was in view, grinned, and waved. Liam's fingers twitched, wanting to wave back, even though Felix couldn't see him.

He practically drooled as Felix moved to the massage chair, thrusting his arse out towards the camera and shaking it before sitting down. He'd claim that arse soon enough. Felix sat with his knees bent and his legs splayed, everything proudly on display. Liam sucked in a shuddering breath as he stared at the beautiful sight. Felix wasn't hard yet, unlike Liam, but he was still gorgeous. The boy squeezed some lube into his hand and then grasped his cock to smear it over his length.

"Cold," Felix said in a shivering whisper. His mouth twitched into a nervous smile. "I hope this is okay," he said. "It's weird without you here, Daddy."

It was good that Felix was being honest. They could talk about the boy's full experience afterwards.

Felix stared directly into the camera as he worked his cock, occasionally licking his lips, which made them glisten. Liam was mesmerised. It was so much easier to take in the entirety of Felix on the screen than in person, and his boy was putting on a wonderful show. The nervousness he'd displayed in the first seconds seemed to fade as he pleasured himself. At one point, Felix's wet fingers roamed from his cock to his arse, teasing over his entrance. Liam tensed, wondering if Felix was going to be naughty, but he didn't push a finger inside himself. It had been a teasing gesture, Liam decided.

As Felix's eyes began to flutter open and shut and his breaths became shallow pants, Liam stroked his cock, which was leaking and sensitive as a result of watching the young man. It wouldn't take much to tip over the edge, but he wanted to wait for Felix to come. He wanted to enjoy the moment of climax with his boy.

"Daddy," Felix whimpered on the screen.

He was still trying to look into the camera, but it was clear he was losing control of himself.

"You're doing great," Liam whispered, even though Felix couldn't hear him.

He'd tell Felix that when they were together again. He'd shower him with praise and kisses. He'd never seen anyone look so beautiful or perfect as they were about to climax. It was even more wonderful than when he'd had Felix on his knees that morning in the garden. He grunted as he felt his orgasm building, gritting his teeth to keep it at bay just a little longer. He couldn't tear his stare away from the screen. Not that he wanted to.

"Daddy!" Felix cried out as his body was racked by orgasmic convulsions, and cum spurted from his cock.

Liam let himself go then, cum spilling over his hand and onto his bed as he panted and grunted through his orgasm—the best he'd had in longer than he cared to think about.

On the screen, Felix's skin was flushed a bright shade of pink. He was lolling on the massage chair, his cum-covered hand lying limply over his equally messy stomach. His legs were still splayed wide. He took deep breaths and licked his lips, over and over. Liam hoped the boy's orgasm had been as hard and satisfying as his own. It certainly looked like it had been.

"I… hope…" Felix dragged in a breath. "Can't talk," he laughed. "Can't think." He raised his hand and then let it drop again. "Fuck that was good." His stare found the camera again. "I hope that was good for you too," he managed. "I'm just gonna…" He pointed to the bed. "Take a nap." He grinned sleepily at the camera. "Feel free to come over and join me." He rolled onto the bed, curling up on his side.

Even that was beautiful, and Liam watched Felix for some time, feeling sleepy and deeply satisfied himself.

Eventually he roused himself to clean up and get dressed. He kept checking on the screen, but Felix seemed to be fast asleep. His breathing was deep and even, his body relaxed. Even sleeping, he was smiling.

Liam felt a tug in his gut as he closed the laptop lid and went downstairs to throw them some lunch together. It was nothing fancy, just cold cuts of meat and salad in sandwiches. He added a plate of biscuits to the tray, knowing Felix would need something sweet and sugary to help replenish his energy, then covered the tray with foil and carried it next door. He'd left the door on the latch when he'd left earlier, so was able to let himself in rather than knocking, so he didn't disturb Felix.

After dropping the tray of food off in the kitchen and taking some time to fuss the puppy, Liam went upstairs. Felix was lying exactly where he had been when Liam had stopped watching the feed. He turned that off first and then sat down on the bed beside his boy, gently stroking his shoulder.

"You came," Felix said sleepily, half twisting so he could smile and stare up at Liam.

"We both did."

Felix laughed. "Was what I did okay?" he asked, his brow furrowing.

"It was perfect." Liam leant down to press a gentle kiss to Felix's mouth. "*You* were perfect."

Felix's forehead smoothed out again, replaced by a sunshine smile.

"I thought you were going to be naughty," Liam said, making his voice sterner.

"I thought about it. But…" Felix's cheeks flushed red. "But then realised I don't want anything inside me except you either."

Warmth flooded through Liam, pulsing straight to his groin. He lay down beside Felix and wrapped the boy in his arms. Felix snuggled against him.

"Was it good for you?" Liam asked, kissing the top of the boy's head over and over, just as he'd promised himself he would.

"Yes," Felix whispered. "I was nervous, and it was weird not having you there, but once I got into it…" He whistled softly. "It was hot, Daddy."

Liam kissed his way down Felix's face to his mouth. "I'm glad you enjoyed yourself."

The minutes blurred as they kissed and held each other.

"I've brought lunch," Liam said eventually, even though he could have happily stayed there, with Felix in his arms, for the rest of the day.

"The only thing I'm hungry for is you," Felix whined, rubbing against him.

"You need to eat," Liam said sternly. "You skipped breakfast."

"Fuck me first?" Felix pleaded. He ran his fingers through Liam's beard. "Then I'll eat a whole fucking cow if you want me to."

"Just sandwiches." Liam chuckled. "And biscuits." He stroked Felix's face. "We're going to have lunch, *now*."

Felix pouted, but Liam refused to allow his resolve to be rocked.

"Lunch," he repeated, disentangling himself from Felix's needy body. "Get dressed. I'll see you downstairs in a few minutes."

18

FELIX

Felix cleaned himself up but didn't get dressed. He waltzed downstairs and swaggered into the dining room, as naked as the day he was born.

Liam was sitting at the table, lunch neatly arranged in front of him. It looked delicious, reminding Felix that he was, in fact, hungry. Not that he was going to let a little thing like a growling stomach detract him from teasing Liam. He put a bottle of lube and a box of condoms on the far end of the table.

"Just in case," he said with a nonchalant shrug when Liam glared at him.

"I told you to get dressed," Liam said disapprovingly.

"Did you?" Felix pressed his forefinger against his lips. "I must not have heard you."

"You heard."

Felix grinned. "You're right, I did. Maybe you should punish me?" He turned around and bent over slightly, presenting his arse to Liam for a spanking.

Disappointment flooded him when Liam didn't strike him. He stood tall and faced him. Liam stared at him sternly, his gigantic arms crossed over his broad chest.

"Have you finished making a spectacle of yourself?" Liam demanded. "Go and put some clothes on."

"Why?" Felix challenged. "Am I too hard to resist when I'm naked?"

"Put your clothes on."

Felix lifted his chin. "No."

Liam growled deep in his throat. "You're being very naughty," he warned.

"I am?" Felix gasped. "Really?"

Liam's eyes narrowed. He pushed his chair back, but instead of standing, he patted his lap as though he was inviting Felix to sit there. Without hesitation, Felix approached him, but before he had a chance to sit, Liam grabbed him by the wrist and shoulder and put him over his lap. Felix let out a sound that was somewhere between a giggle and a cry of surprise. The blood rushed to his head as he lay over Liam's lap, arse up. He was certain he was going to get spanked.

He wasn't wrong.

Liam's hand came down on his arse hard, making his body jerk and a small cry tear out of his throat. He balled his hands into tight fists as Liam struck him again, even harder. His arse stung and felt hot already. When Liam didn't immediately hit him again, he wiggled in the big man's lap, rubbing his hard cock against Liam's leg. His 'reward' was another, harder, slap. Then he felt a different sensation. A sharp, localised pain in his right butt cheek. Was Liam pinching him? He yelped as Liam did it again and again in a slightly different spot, keeping him guessing as to where the pain would come from.

"You need to be patient, boy," Liam hissed.

"I'm not good at being patient," Felix pointed out. It was his way of begging for more.

Instead, Liam stroked his arse, the soft, gentle pressure a harsh juxtaposition to the pain he'd inflicted seconds earlier.

"I could give you what you want," Liam mused. "I could fuck you over the table right now while your arse is red and sore."

"Please," Felix whispered.

Liam pinched him again, hard enough to make him yelp.

"But what sort of lesson would I be teaching you?"

Felix scrabbled to come up with a good answer, one that would result in him getting fucked over the table.

"I wouldn't be teaching you patience," Liam said. "If anything, I would be rewarding bad behaviour. I told you to get dressed, yet here you are, naked."

He went back to stroking Felix's arse, which of course turned Felix on even more. He wasn't sure he could take any more frustration before he jizzed all over Liam's jeans.

"Because I want you," he said. "And I know you want me too."

"And then you lied, telling me you hadn't heard me," Liam went on, seemingly ignoring Felix's statement.

"I was very naughty," Felix agreed impatiently. "But

you've punished me for that." He wiggled his arse beneath Liam's hand.

"Who says I've finished?" Liam asked.

The warmth of his hand vanished from Felix's arse. He barely had time to catch his breath before Liam's hand slammed down on his flesh again. He cried out and then bit his lip, wondering, for the first time, if he should use one of his safe words, but he didn't really want the punishment to stop. He was enjoying it too much despite the pain. He felt two different kinds of warmth in his body: the stinging heat from being slapped and the delicious, all-consuming warmth of an impending orgasm.

"You're a very." Liam struck him again. "Naughty." Another slap, the hardest yet, the sound reverberating in Felix's ears. "Boy."

When Liam struck him again, Felix came. His body shuddered over and over, almost beyond control. He felt his cum between his body and Liam's jeans, hot and sticky. Liam stroked his arse as he gradually recovered. He felt tired but happy, sated and yet still ridiculously frustrated because as wonderful as *that* orgasm had been, he still wanted Liam inside him.

"You've made a mess of me, boy," Liam chastised.

Felix wanted to point out that it was Liam's fault for making him come, but instead he whispered, "I'm sorry, Daddy." And then a wickedly naughty thought popped into his mind and spilt out his mouth. "I guess you'll just have to take your clothes off too."

He was expecting the slap that followed, but it still

stung like hell. It didn't put him off. He carried on down that path, like an out of control train.

"You probably need a shower too. We could take one together, and you could fuck me against the tiles."

"You recover quickly from orgasms, don't you?" he asked in a thoughtful tone.

Felix shrugged. "It's a natural gift, I guess."

Or a curse because none of his previous boyfriends had been happy that he was able to get hard again faster than them. But Liam was different. He seemed to get pleasure out of making Felix come or watching him have an orgasm.

"It's a gift you could take advantage of right now," he ventured.

"Oh?"

"Take me upstairs right now and fuck me in the shower. We could come together. It would be sexy as hell, don't you think?"

"Do you want me to spank you again?" Liam asked.

Yes. No. Maybe? Felix's brain was still fogged from his orgasm. His arse hurt, but he was pretty sure he could take more if Liam chose to keep spanking him. But what he really wanted was to do was explore how their naked bodies fit together. There was a substantial size difference between them, height and bulk, more than he'd experienced with any other man. He wanted to feel every inch of Liam against him and in him. His body was so needy that he knew he'd endure anything if sex was his reward at the end of it. He'd *never* felt so desperate for a man before. But that had been the point in Liam teaching him to have patience, hadn't it? He understood now that when they finally fucked, his release would probably be more intense than anything he had ever felt before. He'd thought his orgasms over the last few days had been great—he definitely hadn't known he could come as a result of being spanked—but he was now convinced they'd pale in comparison to what he'd feel when he came with Liam inside him.

"I'll wait, Daddy," he said, his voice little more than a pitiful rasp. "I'll be patient."

"Good boy," Liam said soothingly, rubbing gentle circles over Felix's arse cheeks.

They stayed like that for a few more minutes, Felix hanging limply as he enjoyed the sensation of Liam's palm massaging his flesh and the stickiness of his cum, which seemed to cement him to his lover. The heat of their bodies had kept it warm, but it would start to cool soon and then it would feel a lot less sexy.

"You can get up now," Liam told him.

Felix obeyed, though he needed Liam's help to get upright again, and his legs felt wobbly beneath him.

"Clean up and then come back to have your lunch."

Felix was pretty certain Liam hadn't ordered him to put clothes on. Clean up. Come back. That definitely didn't involve getting dressed.

He went to the kitchen to wash himself down. Domino greeted him, giving him a confused look at first. The puppy was probably wondering why his human was naked. After cleaning up, Felix scratched Domino behind the ears for a couple of minutes before giving the puppy his lunch. Then he returned to the dining room.

Liam hadn't touched the food, though he had pulled his chair back in. He didn't comment on Felix's state of undress at all, although his lusty stare did slide up and down Felix's body. Felix sat down, wincing at how tender his arse felt. He started to stand but froze when Liam gave him a withering stare. Being uncomfortable while he ate was obviously going to be part of his punishment. He sat back down and began to eat.

He fidgeted through the whole meal. By the time Liam handed a biscuit to him, he was glad for the sugar. He was tired and sore but also insanely happy. Logically, he knew it was because the spanking and the orgasm had released a burst of endorphins into his system, but emotionally he knew it was because of Liam. The man made him happy. He felt cared for. He wasn't just a prize to fuck and leave. The attention Liam gave him— all of it—made him feel wanted.

When they'd finished eating, Liam began to clear the plates. Felix went to help him but was stopped by a glare. He stayed put, rocking from arse cheek to arse cheek so he didn't put too much pressure on any one point for more than a few seconds. When Liam stood, he saw the white stain on the man's dark jeans, caused by his cum. Not that he felt guilty about it, and he *had* suggested that Liam take them off.

"Go upstairs," Liam said, holding the small stack of plates and cutlery. "Take a shower."

Felix frowned but decided not to question or argue. He might have thought he could take more of a spanking earlier, but now he knew he couldn't. He stood and trudged up the stairs, wanting to sleep more than shower, wondering whether Liam would still be downstairs when he'd finished or the man would have gone home.

Felix was about to get out of the shower when the bathroom door opened and Liam entered the room, grimacing.

"It's ugly, isn't it?" Felix laughed. "I'm planning on getting it ripped out and replaced."

"Good."

Liam leant against the door frame, staring at him. He wasn't sure whether he should get out of the shower or stay put. He wanted Liam to tell him what to do, so he stood there, letting the water pour over him, staring back at his lover.

Without a word, Liam started to get undressed. He took his top off first, taking Felix's breath away with the size of his muscles. He'd heard the term 'washboard stomach' before, but that wasn't sufficient. For some reason, he hadn't expected Liam to wax his chest, but it was clear he did.

Liam's socks came off next, probably the most boring things he could have taken off. When Liam unfastened the button on his jeans, Felix bit his lip. He followed the slow movement of Liam's hand as he pulled the zipper down, and could barely breathe as Liam pushed the jeans down his tree trunk legs and stepped out of them. Felix wasn't sure how it was possible, but Liam looked *bigger* without clothes on. He decided it was because he could see the definition of Liam's bulging muscles. The sight was definitely making him weak at the knees.

Finally, Liam pulled his underwear down.

"Oh, God," Felix moaned as his stare feasted on Liam's thick and long cock.

It had sprung up as soon as it had been freed, jutting proudly away from Liam's body and the mass of dark crotch hair. Felix's hands moved to cup his own cock, which suddenly seemed inferior in comparison.

"Don't," Liam ordered. "You're beautiful."

"You're—" Felix blew out a breath and reached out to lean against the wall. It was the only way he was going to stay standing. He couldn't put into words how glorious Liam looked.

He hadn't expected Liam to come upstairs at all. When he'd started to get undressed, it had been clear that he hadn't just come up to the bathroom to watch Felix shower, which left him confused as hell because his arse still stung from being taught a lesson about patience. Yet here Liam was, naked and walking towards him.

His body shook with anticipation as Liam stepped into the bath. Gently, Liam turned Felix round and then pressed his body against Felix's back. His muscles were hard and unyielding, and Felix swore he could feel the outline of every single one pushed up against him. Liam's cock rubbed over his sore arse, making Felix groan and tip his head back against his lover's chest. Liam's arms snaked around him, one hand playing with his left nipple, the other stroking his cock.

"Have I told you how amazing you were earlier?" Liam asked before kissing Felix's neck, just below his ear. His damp beard tickled Felix's skin. "When I was watching you?"

Felix nodded, unable to speak. His eyes fluttered shut. The only thing he was capable of doing was feeling Liam and everything he was doing to his desperate body.

"You made me so happy," Liam whispered.

He nibbled Felix's ear, occasionally nipping hard enough to cause a small burst of pain. Felix melted against him, only standing because Liam wouldn't let him fall. He wondered if this was the moment Liam would decide to take him, but he quickly reined his thoughts in. This was probably another lesson in patience, a wonderfully sexy lesson that he was going to pay a lot of attention to.

Liam's hand moved from his cock to stroke his arse. "Your arse is so red," he murmured. His nibbling kisses moved to Felix's collarbone. "It's sexy."

Felix shuddered with delight and pressed back against Liam's hand.

"Does it hurt?"

"A little."

Liam rubbed him soothingly. "I promised you a reward once you'd finished reading the script."

Felix frowned. "I thought I'd had it, Daddy." Hadn't that been what the camera was all about?

Liam chuckled, the happy movement of his chest jostling Felix. He pinched Felix's nipple between his fingers, making Felix swear under his breath. Then he let go and stepped back. Cold air rushed between them, and even the warmth of the shower couldn't make up for the gaping loss that Felix felt. He whimpered but didn't object or turn around. He stood there, using the wall to prop himself up, trusting that Liam was about to do something wonderful.

He heard the squeak of the bath behind him, and then Liam's hands clutched his hips tightly. Felix quivered, his pulse picking up as Liam peppered his arse with tender kisses. Then Liam's tongue slid down his crack. Felix's arms shook with the effort of keeping upright as Liam's big strong hands parted his arse cheeks. He almost came undone when he felt Liam's tongue lap around his entrance, hot and urgent. His knees went completely when Liam's tongue pushed inside him, but the bigger man managed to keep him on his feet. How, Felix wasn't sure, nor was his mind in any state to figure it out, as Liam's tongue worked in and out of him.

To his embarrassment, it only took seconds for Liam to bring him to the brink of an orgasm and then send him crashing over the edge. Liam's tongue continued to pillage him as he shook through it, cum spurting onto the tiles, only to get washed away instantly. He panted through each climactic wave, not sure how Liam was capable of producing such ecstasy.

Liam stood and wrapped Felix's orgasm-wrecked body into his arms. "Did you like that?"

"Yes," Felix breathed. "So, so much."

It had made him want to take Liam's cock even

more, a desire which wasn't helped by the fact that he could feel it pressing against him.

Liam reached around him and turned off the shower. Then he lifted Felix into his arms and out of the bath. He grabbed towels for them both, wrapping Felix up before drying himself. Felix watched spellbound as Liam rubbed the towel over himself. Once he was dry, he discarded the towel and finished drying Felix. The air had done a fairly good job, but Felix wasn't going to complain about Liam's hands rubbing roughly all over him, even if a towel did separate Liam's skin from his. When he was done, Liam threaded his fingers through Felix's and led him out of the room. Neither of them had clothes on, Felix realised, his mind finally kicking back into gear, and they were going into his bedroom.

19

LIAM

When they went into the bedroom, Felix stopped and stared at the tray that Liam had put on the table built into Felix's bed. Liam had used the tray to bring up a glass of milk, the rest of the plate of biscuits from lunch, and the lube and box of condoms that Felix had brashly brought down to the dining room before lunch. Felix looked up at him, eyebrows quirked in confusion.

Liam explained nothing as he steered the boy onto the bed. He didn't need to explain his change of heart to Felix. He only had to justify it to himself. He'd warred with himself while he'd been clearing up, but the truth was that everything had changed the moment Felix had promised to be patient in such a genuinely heartfelt manner. It had wrenched at Liam's heart, and he'd known the boy had understood the lesson he'd been trying to teach him for the last few days.

He wrapped himself around Felix, his massive body almost swallowing the boy's up. Even then, lying naked together, their bodies still hot from the shower, Liam warred with himself over his decision to take their relationship to the next level. He had told Felix he had to learn to be patient, yet here *he* was, about to let go of every ounce of self-control he had. He could still pull back and claim he was teaching Felix another lesson by dangling the tantalising promise of sex right before his nose, only to snatch it away again. After all, in the shower, he'd given Felix his reward for reading the script. But he wasn't a jerk. He wasn't going to be cruel for the sake of it. He'd made Felix—and himself—wait long enough.

It was hard not to moan when Felix began to run his hands over his body in a tender, exploratory fashion.

"You're so amazing," Felix whispered, sounding utterly awestruck.

Felix's chin started to quiver, and his eyes became bright with tears. Liam's chest ached at the thought the boy might be upset or unhappy.

Gently, he tipped Felix's chin up. "What's wrong, boy?"

"Nothing," Felix sniffed.

"Tell me," Liam ordered. There was no way he was letting him get away with the obvious lie. Besides, if he didn't know what was wrong, he couldn't make it better.

"It's just…" Felix shrugged and swiped at his eyes. "I'm a bit overwhelmed."

"What by?"

"You. *Us.*" Felix glanced down at Liam's crotch, and he swallowed hard before clearing his throat, his cheeks flushing a bright shade of pink. "The way I feel about you… It's crazy." He shook his head. "I'm sorry."

"Why are you sorry?"

Liam's heart was pattering. It hadn't done that in response to anyone in far too long—since before he took early retirement and turned his back on a world he'd convinced himself was rotten to the core—but nothing about Felix was rotten. He was nothing but sweetness and light, wrapped up in a sassy and often exhausting bundle.

"For getting too heavy too quickly." Felix waved his hand. "Ignore me. I'm being ridiculous."

He tried to roll away, but Liam didn't let him.

"Tell me how you feel," Liam commanded. He needed to know.

Felix shook his head.

"Tell me," Liam growled.

Felix stared at him and then wriggled his arse, which had to still be tender from the decisive spanking Liam had given him.

"I'm falling in love with you," Felix admitted in a hushed whisper. He stared deep into Liam's eyes as he carried on. "No one has ever made me feel the way I do with you. And I know it's too fast and too soon and that I'm being ridiculous, so you can ignore every word I've just said and pretend I didn't. I don't want anything to change between us, just because I can't keep my silly thoughts to myself."

Every rushed word hit Liam like a mini tidal wave, each one leaving him reeling more than the last. It wasn't exactly a declaration of love, but it came pretty damned close.

"Are you finished?" he asked when Felix paused to breathe.

The boy nodded. Liam kissed him, hard and long, using his tongue to explore Felix's mouth in the same way he'd used it to tease and pleasure the boy's arse. The kiss was both to show Felix that he wasn't going to ignore his ramble and to give himself time to think. Felix trembled beneath him, his hands stroking every inch of skin they could reach. Liam kept kissing Felix until the tension he'd felt in the boy's body while he'd been pouring his heart out had fully melted away.

When the kiss ended, Felix's lips were damp and swollen, and his face was red from where Liam's beard had rubbed against it. It was definitely satisfying for Felix's arse and face to be red because of him. Although Felix had relaxed, there was still worry in his wide eyes. Liam's chest ached, and he knew he needed to give the boy more reassurance than a kiss.

"I haven't let myself care about anyone in a long time," he admitted. "I haven't taken on a boy in years." He hadn't wanted to either. "But you... You're stunning." He stroked Felix's hair, buying himself some time to find the right words to explain how Felix had changed everything with his infuriating behaviour. It felt almost triumphant when the right ones came to him. "I hadn't realised my life had got so overcast until you burst into it. I wasn't looking for anyone, but now I've found you I don't want to let you go." It wasn't exactly a declaration of love either, but, like Felix's words, it was pretty damned close.

Felix whimpered, laughed, and cried all at the same time. It was a happy sound that made Liam's heart and groin pulse with pleasure. Oh, he was definitely done waiting. He reached for the bottle of lube. Felix pressed his hands over his face, making Liam worry.

"Do you still want me inside you?" he asked. He would have held his breath while he waited for the response, but Felix spoke too quickly for him to need to.

"Yes," he whispered, lowering his hands far enough that he could peep over his fingertips. "So, so much."

Liam frowned. "Then why are you crying?"

"Because I'm happy. I don't think I've ever felt this happy."

"Then stop crying," Liam ordered. "Laugh if you want, but I don't want my boy to cry while we make love."

Felix sniffed back his tears and then let out an ecstatic laugh. The sound was wild, filling the room. His body, still pressed against Liam's, quivered with anticipation as Liam squeezed some lube onto his fingers. The lube was cold, making Felix shiver as Liam's fingers made contact with his arse, but it warmed up quickly as Liam stroked, teased, and then slipped one thick finger slowly inside the boy. Felix gasped and arched his back, laughing again as Liam thrust his finger back and forth. Hot, swirling, pressure built up in Liam's cock, and he could only imagine what Felix was feeling. He'd already had three orgasms that day. If the speed of the last one was anything to go by, he was likely to be on the brink already, which simply wouldn't do.

"Need you," Felix said, echoing Liam's thoughts. He wriggled and writhed on Liam's finger. "Oh, fuck, Daddy, I'm not going to be able to hold it in."

"Rule number five?"

"My… orgasms… belong… to… you…" Felix panted. "Daddy, I don't think I can stop it."

"You can and you will," Liam told him in a commanding tone. "You'll come when I tell you to and not before."

"Fuck!" Felix cried out as Liam's finger found his prostate and stroked the area over and over. "That's not fair!"

"What isn't?"

"Telling me not to come while doing *that*."

"Hmmm… Then I suppose this wouldn't be fair?" Liam asked, adding a second slippery finger.

Felix raised his hands above his head, clutching the pillow desperately. "No," he whined. "Not fair at all."

He tossed his head from side to side, probably in an attempt to stave off his need to release. Liam pressed his mouth over Felix's, forcing him to stop his desperate movements. He knew it would make it even harder for Felix to contain his orgasm, but the boy would thank him for it eventually.

"And *this* wouldn't be fair either," he teased, breaking the kiss.

He added a third finger. Felix bared down on his fingers so they sank deeper inside. Beads of sweat began to break out over the boy's skin, making it glisten. Fuck, he was sexy as hell. Liam kissed him again, moving his tongue in time with his fingers.

"Need you," Felix gasped when Liam released him from the kiss. "*Now.*"

Liam chuckled. "I want—"

"Doesn't get!" Felix snapped the words out desperately. "*Please*, Daddy. I *need* you."

Liam's insides erupted with heat at the perfect words from a perfect boy.

"Patience, boy."

He kissed Felix again before licking his way down his chest, swirling his tongue around one nipple and then the other. He sucked each nipple into his mouth until they were hard and pert. Felix moaned and whimpered, writhing and thrusting against Liam's fingers, clearly desperate to be fucked.

Liam slipped his fingers free, and Felix laughed desperately. No more waiting. No more teasing. Liam took a condom out of the box and handed it to Felix.

"Put it on me."

Felix sat slowly. His eyes were huge and round, and his hands trembled as he carefully opened the packet and rolled the condom onto Liam's cock. He gulped and looked up. Liam saw desire and worry side by side in Felix's eyes.

"I'll be gentle," Liam promised him. "I'll go slowly. If you need me to stop, tell me." He meant it. He wanted this first time together to be beautiful, not painful.

Smiling, Felix went to lie back down, but Liam caught him by the shoulder, stopping him.

"Swap places."

Felix frowned but obeyed. Liam settled himself so he was sitting with his back resting against the headboard. He motioned for Felix to come to him, and guided him into a straddle position on his knees.

"Now you're in control," Liam told him before smiling. "For now."

He grabbed the bottle of lube again, slicking his cock up, even though Felix's arse was already damp and slippery from their foreplay. He took hold of Felix's hips, and they stared into each other's eyes.

"Whenever you're ready."

Felix swiped his tongue over his lips. In the seconds that followed, a range of emotions flickered over his face, leaving Liam guessing as to what he was thinking. He remained quiet, doing nothing but make tiny soothing, circular motions over Felix's hips as he let his boy think. Suddenly, Felix's mouth spread into a wide, amused grin as though he were laughing at himself internally. He seemed to relax, though he still didn't move. Liam lifted his hips far enough to brush the bulbous head of his cock against Felix, making the boy shiver. In response, Felix lowered himself a little. Liam felt the tight ring of muscle at Felix's entrance push against the head of his cock. It was fucking amazing, and he had to actively stop himself from losing control and thrusting up. He'd promised Felix control for this part, and he wouldn't take it away.

Felix breathed in deeply, releasing a slow breath as he pushed down a bit farther. His eyebrows twitched together. Liam made soothing sounds, applying more pressure as he continued to rub Felix's hips.

"Take all the time you need. There's no need to rush."

Felix took another breath and pressed down farther, his muscles relaxing enough to allow the head of Liam's cock to sink inside him. Liam watched the boy's face carefully, relieved when his eyebrows pulled apart again. Felix sank down slowly, inch by inch, breathing deeply, as his hot muscles pulsed around Liam's cock. Their gazes remained locked, and Liam kept stroking Felix and making soothing sounds. Once Felix's arse rested against Liam's balls, he leant forward and placed his head on Liam's shoulder.

"Okay?" Liam asked.

Felix nodded. "You're just so *big*."

"And you're so tight and hot," Liam said. "We can stay like this as long as you like. We can stop if—"

"No!" Felix cried. "God, no. I don't want to stop."

"Good."

Felix lifted his head and stroked Liam's face. "Fuck me, Daddy," he urged. "Fuck me hard."

Liam grinned wider than he had in a long time, so wide his cheek muscles ached from the effort. His body overflowed with lust combined with a purer and more powerful emotion. He pushed his hips up, driving his cock deeper into Felix.

Felix arched his back and neck, gasping as Liam filled him completely. Shaking, he flopped forward again, resting his forehead against Liam's. Liam ignored the slight sting of pain as Felix's fingers clutched at his hair.

He made love to the boy slowly at first. Each thrust a little deeper than the last. Tears leaked from Felix's eyes and slid down his cheeks, but he was smiling and looked genuinely happy, so Liam tenderly kissed them away. He was glad he'd forced them both to wait. As a result, their union wasn't solely about lust. Felix began to move his body in harmony with Liam's, which heightened Liam's pleasure. Felix arched back again, his hands moving from Liam's hair to clutch his shoulders tightly as their lovemaking became faster. They both grunted out hard breaths, and their skin became damp with sweat. Liam stared at Felix, entranced. Golden afternoon sunlight poured into the room, bathing Felix's body in its radiance, making his sweat-bejewelled skin glisten as though the light was bursting out from inside him.

"Sunshine," Liam gasped on an upwards thrust. "You're made of sunshine, beautiful boy."

"I'm *your* boy, Daddy," Felix whispered.

"*My* boy," Liam agreed, his voice rumbling straight from his heart.

He wiped damp strands of hair away from Felix's forehead and then dragged him close for a kiss before rolling them both over, so Felix was on his back. Felix wrapped his legs around him. Liam's fingers twisted into Felix's as he drove into him urgently and relentlessly. Their lips were a breath apart, but Liam didn't kiss him. Their desperate breaths made the air hot between them.

"Don't close your eyes," Liam barked out when Felix's eyes threatened to flicker shut.

Felix opened his eyes wide, and they stared at each other once more. The moment was so intimate, so intense, that Liam felt like he was staring straight into Felix's brilliant soul and that the boy was staring straight into his.

"Come," he ordered, unable to contain himself any longer.

Felix cried out as his body was racked with one violent shudder after another. Jets of his cum hit Liam in the stomach. Liam grunted and moaned as his body shook and his cock pulsed deep inside Felix. Their orgasms seemed to last forever. Liam thrust through each wave that hit him, deeper and deeper. By the time the last ripples of his orgasm had ebbed away, he was exhausted.

Felix panted beneath him, still staring up into his eyes. Even though Liam was spent, he wanted to stay inside his boy for as long as possible. It seemed Felix wanted that too because he reached up, tugged Liam down, and wrapped his arms around his back.

"Thank you," he whispered into Liam's ear. "For making me wait. For teaching me patience. For being gentle. Thank you for everything."

"You're *my* boy," Liam told him firmly and gently, his voice breaking with overwhelming happiness. "I will *always* take care of you."

20

FELIX

"So?" Rick asked. "How's it going with your neighbour?"

"Good!"

Felix sat on the sitting room floor, using a figure-eight-shaped chew toy to play tug with Domino as he talked to Rick. He'd turned the speakerphone mode on, which made it easier to interact with the bright-eyed puppy. It was a hot day, and the north-facing rooms were only just bearable with all the windows open. He definitely missed air con but knew it was too much of a luxury for the few truly hot days the UK was blessed with.

"I need more than that," Rick said. "Were you aggressive?"

"I did yoga in my garden, wearing those shorts you bought me."

Rick cackled down the phone. "Okay, yeah, *that's* aggressive. Did he take the bait?"

"Yeah," Felix breathed. "He did."

"Go on."

"I'm not giving you all the details."

"You're no fun."

Felix could imagine his friend pouting, which made him chuckle.

"You've got to give me something," Rick objected. "Has he spanked you yet?"

"Yes." Felix adjusted his position. His arse was still a tiny bit tender from the dining room spanking the day before. "He likes me to call him Daddy."

He let Domino win their game. Not that he'd been trying hard as he didn't want the puppy to hurt his teeth. Domino immediately brought the toy back to him, and their game began again, the puppy making all kinds of funny growling noises as it tried to tug the toy free of Felix's grip.

"Are you good with that?" Rick asked.

"Yeah, I am."

"You sound happy."

Felix snorted softly. "How can you tell?"

"You've barely strung four words together all phone call."

"Shut up," Felix mumbled, but he was grinning inanely.

Liam *did* make him happy on so many levels.

"It takes a lot to shut the great Felix Lee up," Rick went on. "You're going to have to give me your Daddy Dom's phone number so he can tell me what his secret is."

"You're an idiot."

He let go of the toy again, giving Domino his fifth victory in a row. This time the puppy left the toy on the floor and came to flop down beside Felix, his chin resting on his thigh.

"I'm glad he's making you happy, Felix," Rick said. "You deserve it."

Felix's sappy grin became even wider. A sigh escaped him as he stroked Domino. The last week or so had been a wildly different pace of life than the one he'd been used to for most of his life, but it was a welcome one, and Liam was definitely a good addition.

"You need to tell me all about him," Rick went on. "I need *all* the details, including a description that's vivid enough I can wank over it."

"Hey!" Felix objected. "He's mine. Find someone else to fantasise about."

Rick laughed. "I think you'll find you're *his* rather than the other way around. You're his boy, right?"

"Yes," Felix breathed. The happiness inside him grew a little more, making him feel even hotter.

"So come on, tell me all about him."

Felix rubbed Domino under his chin, which made the puppy pant and give him an adorably cute look. He wasn't sure which he'd miss most when he went to the States for a few days for his audition, Liam or Domino. Emma hadn't got back to him with any details yet, so he shoved the thought aside.

"Felix?"

"I…" Felix frowned. "I don't really know that much

about him." That was something he was going to have to remedy.

"You must know *something* if you're calling him Daddy and letting him spank you."

"He makes me smile," Felix said. "And laugh. He makes me feel safe and wanted."

"He turns you on."

"Obviously. He used to be a police detective but took early retirement, and now he grows roses."

"Early retirement? Jesus, Felix, how old *is* this guy?"

"I dunno… mid to late forties? I haven't asked because it doesn't bother me."

"Hey, all power to you," Rick said. "But… uh… A guy who potters around growing roses really doesn't seem like your type. You're used to the fast life, Felix. It's not going to be long before you want to get back to going out clubbing and to parties every night of the week."

"I'm not missing it," Felix assured him.

"*Yet*. I hope this guy of yours knows you'll be jetting off on him as soon as a film role catches your eye."

"We've only been seeing each other for a few days. You're making it sound like we're thinking about exchanging marriage vows already."

"I know you, Felix," Rick said softly. "You have this habit of making people fall in love with you, whether you mean to or not. All I'm saying is that you need to be careful. Make sure his expectations for the future are realistic. *We* both know you won't be sticking around in that quaint little house of yours for more than a few months."

Felix wasn't sure he *did* know that. His gut twisted. He *had* agreed to an audition. Maybe Rick was right, and that, deep down, this *wasn't* the life he wanted long term. Just thinking about it smothered a little of the happiness that had been glowing brightly inside of him since Liam had made love to him. It didn't matter whether they'd only been together for a few days. The last thing he wanted to do was lead Liam on or give him false promises.

Domino yawned and stretched before settling down again. Felix smiled, but his amusement at the puppy was tinged by the sadness that was starting to creep in at the edges thanks to Rick and his big mouth. It had been selfish of him to get a puppy. He couldn't take Domino to film sets with him. Aside from the fact that flying and weeks in quarantine would be stressful and unfair, he wouldn't have the time to look after a dog, let alone the space in trailers, hotel rooms, or temporary apartments. Nor could he easily leave the dog behind for any length of time. Liam had offered to look after Domino while he auditioned, but a few days was different than a few months.

"You've gone very quiet on me. You okay?" Rick asked.

"Yeah. You just got me thinking."

"In a bad way or a good way?"

Felix sighed. "I don't know yet."

What he did know was that he had some serious, potentially life-altering decisions to make. Decisions that mattered. Decisions that he wasn't used to making.

"I have to go," he told Rick. "Good chat."

"Fe—"

Felix hung up the call. In order to help him make those far too serious decisions, he needed to know more about the grumpy bear he was rapidly falling in love with, and he knew the perfect way to do it.

21

LIAM

"Hi, neighbour," Felix said cheerfully when Liam opened the door.

He was holding a plastic mixing bowl against his chest, with several folded up pieces of paper, and a wine bottle and two glasses in the other hand.

"Hi," Liam said, frowning as he stared from bowl to wine and back again.

"Are you up for playing a game?" Felix asked, barging into the house.

"No."

Felix turned on his best puppy dog eyes. Liam was starting to hate that look on Felix's face because it was too damned hard to resist.

"What game?" Liam asked, even though he was sure he'd regret it.

"Twenty-one questions." Felix tipped his head as he looked at the bowl. "There are loads more than twenty-one in here, so I guess it's more a game of as many as we can get through before we finish the wine." He winked at Liam.

"Isn't that a game teenagers play?" Liam muttered.

"I want to get to know you better, and I thought this would be a fun way to do it." Felix marched off towards the lounge.

Liam glanced up at the ceiling, wondering despairingly what sort of evening he was in for.

"Or we could just talk," he said as he followed Felix. "Like adults."

"Where would be the fun in *that*?" Felix asked as he put the bowl, wine, and glasses down on the coffee table. "Do you have a corkscrew?"

"Kitchen."

Felix stared at him, smiling.

"I'm not your slave," Liam growled. "Get it yourself."

"But you promised to take care of me, Daddy," Felix teased. "I carried the heavy bottle of wine over here. Surely the least you could do is get the corkscrew?"

"You're annoying."

"So you keep telling me." Felix's eyes sparkled. "But you still can't keep away from me."

"*You* came *here*."

"Nope. I haven't come here yet. Maybe you can remedy that by the end of the night." He grinned broadly.

Liam let out an exasperated sigh before trudging to the kitchen to retrieve a corkscrew. Felix really was ridiculous at times. Well, most of the time. And yet that ridiculousness kept Liam on his toes and made him smile despite himself. He'd never met anyone quite like Felix.

By the time he got back to the sitting room, Felix had kicked off his flip-flops and was lying stretched out on the sofa, his arms folded behind his head. His T-shirt had tugged up a little, revealing a kissable band of flesh.

"Making yourself comfortable?" Liam asked.

"Yup. Are you going to come and snuggle with me?" Felix wagged his bare feet back and forth as he spoke, reminding Liam of an overenthusiastic puppy.

"Where's the dog?"

"Sleeping. I tired him out playing earlier. Why? Did you want me to bring him round?"

"No."

"Aww, you love him really. No one could fail to love such a cute puppy." Felix spoke in a silly tone, the kind grown-ups used when they were talking to a very young child, normally while pinching that child's cheek.

Liam rolled his eyes.

"You know, if you keep rolling your eyes like that, you're going to give yourself a headache."

"*You* give me a headache."

Felix sat up and patted the sofa. "Come sit down, and I'll give you a head massage."

"You don't know how to give a head massage."

"Sure I do." Felix waggled his fingers. "I promise you'll like it."

Liam shook his head despairingly as he knelt. He popped the cork free of the wine bottle and poured them both half a glass. He wasn't sure whether alcohol would make Felix more subdued or amp up his silliness.

Probably the latter. He handed Felix a glass and took a sip from the other, raising his eyebrows as he tasted the full-bodied wine.

"You didn't think I could pick a good wine, did you?" Felix asked.

"No," Liam admitted.

"And you'd be right." Felix chuckled. "It was a house-warming present from my agent."

That figured. Liam settled in the armchair, cradling the wine glass.

"Let's play," Felix said without giving Liam any time whatsoever to savour the wine or even half a second of blissful silence. "I'll ask first." He rummaged his hand in the bowl before plucking out a piece of paper, holding and unfolding it with one hand. "Oh, this is a good one. Name one film you like to watch over and over again."

"I don't watch films."

Felix gasped. "Really?" He shook his head. "You're messing with me, right?"

"No."

"*Really?*"

"Really."

"I didn't think that was possible. How can you *not* like to watch films? There's literally a film out there for *everyone*." Felix smiled naughtily. "Even grumpy old bears like you."

Liam released a warning growl. There was no way he was going to admit that he was warming to the idea of Felix calling him 'grumpy bear'. Adding *old* in was definitely going too far, though. He was prepared to give Felix another spanking if he was naughty enough.

"Your turn." Felix pushed the bowl towards him.

Liam huffed out a sigh. "This game is stupid." Despite his words, he plucked a piece of paper out of the bowl and opened it. He groaned before reading it out loud. "Are you wearing any underwear right now?"

Felix laughed. "I was hoping that question would come out later. Maybe I should show you the answer."

He stood and undid the button and zipper of his cut-off jeans, opening them just enough that Liam could see a flash of dark pubic hair rather than underwear.

Desire swirled in Liam's groin, and he felt disappointment as Felix did himself back up again.

"My turn," Felix announced, taking another question from the bottom of the bowl.

Liam drank a sizeable gulp of his wine, unsure why he was about to let Felix ask another question instead of ordering him to take off his shorts. Oh yes, he was humouring his boy, or trying to, at least.

"Have you ever broken anyone's heart?" Felix asked.

"No."

Felix raised his eyebrows. "Oh, come on! How can I get to know you better if you're only going to give me monosyllabic answers?"

"No, I haven't."

Felix chuckled. "You're a funny guy when you want to be. You know you need to tell me more. You've *never* been the heartbreaker in a relationship?"

"No," Liam repeated. "Generally we've agreed it was the right time to part."

"Tell me more," Felix pressed.

Liam finished his wine and poured himself another glass. At this rate, he'd finish the rest of the bottle before Felix had even taken a sip.

"My last boy… He walked away from me because I didn't have enough time for him."

"Really?" Felix looked genuinely surprised.

"I worked long hours when I was on active cases," Liam told him. "I came home in bad moods and wanted to be left alone. It wasn't like I could offload onto him because of confidentiality, nor did he deserve to listen to all the crap I had to deal with." He leant forward onto his knees and drank some more wine.

"So he broke your heart?" Felix asked in a soft tone.

"Maybe, a little."

"I'm sorry."

Liam shrugged. "I chose work over him. It was my own fault."

Felix looked away sharply, his expression briefly clouding over before he replaced it with a smile that looked a little fake. "Your turn."

Liam took another question from the top, hoping whatever question he'd picked would bring a genuine smile to Felix's lips. He unfolded the paper and shook his head. "Are these rigged?"

"Why?" Felix asked. "Have you got another naughty one?"

"What do you wear to bed?" Liam asked in a huffy tone.

The game had to be rigged somehow. Why was he being asked all the serious questions, while Felix got away with answering the flirty ones?

Felix beamed at him. "You'll have to invite me to spend the night to find out."

"That's not an answer."

"It's an invitation to find out the answer. Unless you don't really want to know…"

"Ask the next bloody question," Liam snarled.

Felix laughed as he rummaged around in the bowl and took another piece of paper. "Where's the strangest place you've ever had sex? See? Not rigged!"

"I'm a police officer. Anywhere 'strange' is likely to be a public place and therefore illegal."

"You're an *ex*-police officer," Felix reminded him. "Besides, I don't believe for a second you've never had sex anywhere adventurous. You sucked me off in your greenhouse without pause. You *must* have had sex somewhere else exciting. I bet you like the thrill of fucking where you might get caught." He took a slow sip of his wine, staring at Liam as he did so. "That would have been even more exciting while you were on the force."

"Don't be ridiculous."

"I'd let you fuck me somewhere that we might get caught," Felix said salaciously.

Liam drowned his groan with a gulp of wine.

"Well, if you're not going to answer the question, I will," Felix announced. "The strangest place *I've* ever had sex in is the cargo hold of a starship. It was a prop on a film set, obviously," he added.

Liam had to admit that was a pretty strange place to

have sex. He took another question, if only to move the subject along.

"These *are* rigged," he accused. "What do you think is the sexiest thing about yourself?"

Felix drank more of his wine before answering, prompting Liam to top up both of their glasses.

"Right here," Felix said at last, running a finger from the back of his ear down his neck.

Liam frowned.

"If you kiss me there, it makes me squirm. It drives guys nuts."

The sexy way Felix spoke made Liam want to join him on the sofa so he could kiss and caress that delightful strip of skin, but Felix grabbed a question from the bowl before he could move.

"Name one quality you want people to remember you for," Felix asked.

He bounced on the sofa a little as though he wanted to give an answer to the question on Liam's behalf. Liam was tempted to let him, even though the boy would almost certainly say 'grumpiness'. If nothing else, it would give him an excuse to end the stupid game and turn Felix over his knee. He'd spank the boy and then kiss the skin behind his ear and down his neck, enjoying the way Felix squirmed against him.

Even though Liam didn't answer immediately, Felix didn't produce one of his own, forcing Liam to actually consider the question with a degree of seriousness.

"I have a firm hand," he said eventually in an authoritative tone.

"I bet that was useful when you were on the force," Felix said.

"And in the bedroom."

Felix laughed loudly. "And the dining room and the greenhouse!" Somehow, he managed to gulp his wine down despite still laughing. It was a wonder he didn't snort the fruity red liquid out of his nose. "And I'm still betting those *aren't* the most exciting places you've spanked someone or had sex. I bet you're very naughty when you want to be." His eyes grew wide. "Please tell me you're a member of the mile-high club?"

"The what?" Liam shook his head. "That wasn't a question from the bowl, plus it's my turn to ask one."

Felix grinned triumphantly. "I knew you'd enjoy this game."

"I'm not," Liam lied. "I just want to stop you asking ridiculous questions."

"You're just avoiding answering the question because you don't want me to know how naughty you are. You want me to believe you're a grumpy, boring guy, but you're not. You're funny and sexy and naughty."

Liam rolled his eyes hard. He finished his wine and emptied the bottle, topping their glasses up.

"I knew this game would help me get to know you better," Felix said. "Now I know that you're not just a Dom and a voyeur, but you're also an exhibitionist."

"I am not," Liam huffed. "*You're* the exhibitionist." He grabbed a piece of paper from the bowl. "If you were to make dinner for me, what would you prepare?" At last, a question that wasn't related to sex.

"I'd order takeout."

"I wouldn't let you. If I tell you to make dinner for me, that's what you'd do."

"Well, in that case, I'd make you pizza."

"Buying a pizza and putting it in the oven doesn't count as cooking." Clearly, Felix had learnt nothing during their cooking lessons.

"Spag bol?" Felix suggested. "Boiling some pasta and then mixing in a jar of sauce counts, right?"

"No."

"Oh… I guess you won't want me to cook for you, then. Maybe you should cook for me instead." He finished off his wine and put the glass on the coffee table before taking another question. "How old were you when you first French-kissed, and was it any good?"

Liam was done with the game. He put his glass down and stood. It only took one stride to bring him next to the sofa, where he towered over Felix. "I was fourteen."

Felix whistled approvingly.

"As for whether or not I'm any good at it—you tell me."

He knelt on the sofa and smothered Felix's mouth with his own, thrusting his tongue deep into his boy's mouth. He made sure the kiss was long and hard. He wanted Felix's skin to be red and for him to be panting by the time he released his lips. He pushed his hand beneath Felix's T-shirt, sliding it up his lover's skin to his nipple, which he tweaked, pinched, and rolled with his thumb and forefinger. Felix groaned against his mouth, which only made Liam kiss him harder.

When he was finished, Felix *was* panting, and the skin around his mouth *was* red. It was so sexy.

"That was a good kiss," Felix said breathlessly. "But you can't always have been that good a kisser."

"I was," Liam promised him.

"It's my turn to ask a question."

Liam shook his head. "No. The game is over." He ran his fingertips over the skin that Felix had pointed out earlier and then lowered his lips to Felix's ear. "Now," he whispered in a husky tone. "I'm going to make you squirm."

22

FELIX

Felix did squirm. As Liam lavished attention on the sweet spot behind his ear with lips and tongue, he devolved into a writhing wreck.

"You'll make me come if you keep doing that," Felix said between pants.

"Wasn't that what you wanted?" Liam asked. "For me to make you come in my house?"

Felix giggled. "Yes, but I'd rather come with you inside me."

"Why not both?"

Felix arched his back at the suggestion. "No one's ever actually made me come just by kissing me before."

That was all Liam was doing. There was no other contact between them, just Liam's mouth on the side of his neck, working some kind of magic across his skin.

"Is that a challenge?"

The sexy, deep baritone of Liam's voice made Felix melt. It was a good thing he wasn't wearing underwear because his boxer shorts would have just burst on fire.

How could Liam turn him into a gooey, turned-on wreck with his voice and mouth?

"Yes," Felix whispered. "It's definitely a challenge."

"Then I accept."

Liam upped his game, swirling his tongue over a patch of skin, only to nip it a moment later. Then he sucked the tender skin, kissed it, and then moved a few millimetres to begin again. He assaulted Felix with the constant barrage of tickling delight, small bursts of pain, and gentle touches that left him incapable of doing anything but wriggle and moan beneath the bigger man. His body longed for more contact, and he kept arching up to press himself against Liam's hot, hard body, but every time he tried, Liam moved, denying him. Without really thinking about it, Felix went to slip his hand down his jeans to help himself along to the point of climax.

Liam tutted between a suck and a kiss. "No touching."

At the very least, he needed to undo his button and zip to relieve the pressure of his aching cock. "Can't I just—" He began, touching his button, but Liam cut him off.

"No."

Felix gripped the sofa cushions instead. He let his eyes shut, so there was nothing but him and Liam. In the darkness behind his eyelids, he became hyperaware of every touch of Liam's lips, tongue, and teeth. The pain was more intense, but so was the pleasure.

"You'd look sexy as hell in a blindfold," Liam whispered.

Felix sucked in a breath and opened his eyes so he could stare at his lover. "Do you have one?" He doubted Liam would have brought it up if he didn't have *something* he could cover his eyes with.

"Would you wear one?"

"Yes."

"Wait there."

Felix whimpered as Liam left him and the room. His damp neck felt cool without the touch of Liam's hot tongue and warm lips. He brought his hand up but stopped short of touching the area of skin Liam had been working on. Was it red from being bitten?

It didn't take Liam long to come back to him, holding a black blindfold. It was plain and no-nonsense, just like Liam.

"Are you sure?" Liam asked.

Felix loved the way the man checked in with him. "Yes, Daddy."

He lay still while Liam placed the blindfold around his eyes and secured it. "How does that feel?"

"Good."

"Not too tight?"

"No."

"Can you see anything?"

Felix shook his head. It was amazing how dark the blindfold made things, like the middle of a starless, moonless night. With his eyes closed, there had still been some light pressing against his eyelids. Unable to see, even if he wanted to, Felix could do nothing but lie back and feel as Liam went back to teasing his neck. It was even more intense than when he'd closed his eyes. He felt like he was floating in ecstasy. His body was hot and wanting, his cock hard and aching. He longed for Liam to stroke it or for the man to let him touch him it himself, but every time he tried to move his hand to do exactly that, Liam batted it away. Felix's breathing became shallow and thready as need built up within him, throbbing deep in his groin.

"You're almost there, aren't you, boy?" Liam asked in a low, husky tone.

Felix nodded, though he could hardly believe it. Liam carried on his assault on Felix's neck, his bites a little harder than before, his soothing kisses that bit longer, the swirls of his tongue slower and more intricate. Felix lost it completely. He whimpered and begged Liam for more as he came in his shorts.

Liam's mouth found his, smothering his pleas as he rode out the orgasm. Felix had *never* had an orgasm without someone touching his cock or being in his arse before. *Never*. But then, he'd never been with anyone quite like Liam before, older, more experienced, strong and strict yet caring. He'd never looked for those things in a man, but he was hit by the realisation that he needed them. He needed Liam.

"Challenge complete," Liam said smugly.

"I think you cheated," Felix panted.

"Oh?"

"You were meant to make me come just by kissing me. The blindfold was cheating." He raised his hand to push it up so he could see his lover, but Liam caught hold of his fingers, forbidding him from doing so.

"Leave it on," Liam said.

Felix felt Liam unbuttoning his shorts for him. He let the older man take them off and use them to clean him up. When Liam's gentle touch coaxed him to sit up, he did so obediently, raising his arms above his head when he felt the telltale tug on his T-shirt that told him Liam was intending to fully undress him.

"That's better," Liam said approvingly when Felix was naked except for the blindfold. He kissed Felix tenderly, coaxing him down onto the sofa again. "There's so much I want to do with you."

"Tell me." Felix grinned. "Maybe your next challenge should be to make me come just by talking to me."

Liam chuckled. "One day I'll accept that challenge, but not tonight." He brushed his lips over Felix's jaw, his beard tickling Felix's skin. "You've been tied up before, haven't you?"

"Yes. To be spanked. In a club. Do you…" He swallowed. "Do you want to tie me up, Daddy?"

Liam *had* told him he liked tying up his boys, but that conversation felt like it had taken place a lifetime ago.

"Oh, yes." Liam's voice rumbled out of him.

"Will you tie me up so you can spank me?" Felix's heartrate doubled in speed, or it felt that way anyway. His skin tingled, and his insides buzzed.

Liam sucked Felix's lower lip into his mouth, biting down softly before releasing it. "I want you tied up while I fuck you."

"Oh, Daddy," Felix hissed.

"And if you're very lucky, I'll fuck you *and* spank you."

Felix squeaked, which wasn't the sexiest sound he'd ever made. It made Liam laugh, though, a deep sound that resonated through Felix and turned him on even more.

"Please," he said when he was actually able to make a sound that resembled a word instead of desperate, needy sounds. "I'd like that."

"And if you don't?"

"Then I'll let you know. That's why we have safe words."

"Which you haven't used."

"That's because I haven't needed to. You've been taking care of me, Daddy. You seem to know what I need and how much I can take."

Plus, they'd talked about the things they'd done before trying something new. Liam had known Felix had been spanked in clubs. He'd asked if he wanted to be blindfolded, and now he was asking if he'd agree to being tied up. Liam wasn't springing anything on him. He was introducing everything at a slow pace.

"I feel safe with you, Daddy. *You* make me feel safe."

"A good Daddy should."

"Then you're a wonderful Daddy. Now please, tie me up and fuck me."

Liam chuckled. "That almost sounded like a demand, boy. You don't get to make demands, remember?"

"I remember. I'm sorry, Daddy."

Felix wished he could see Liam's face in that

moment. But he couldn't, and he wasn't going to ask for the blindfold to be removed or try to take it off himself. He was happy to be at Liam's mercy. Happy for Liam to do whatever he wanted with him and to him.

"For that naughtiness and for coming around here with no underwear on, I *am* going to spank you. *After* I've tied you up." He took hold of Felix's hand. "Stand up."

Felix stood up as Liam did, allowing his lover to steady him. It was hard to get his bearings and his balance with the blindfold on, so he ended up swaying. He was pretty sure he'd have fallen back onto the sofa—or worse, the floor—if Liam hadn't been there to look after him.

"Let's go upstairs," Liam whispered into his ear. "*That's* where my toys are."

"Toys?" Felix asked. "You mean you have more than blindfolds and…" He faltered, wondering what Liam would tie him up with. "Handcuffs?" he ventured. It would make sense for Liam to have handcuffs. He had been a police officer.

"I have lots of toys."

Felix sagged as his knees went weak.

Liam steadied him. "But most of them are for me to use on my boy. To pleasure or punish you."

"Are you sure you're not trying to use nothing but words to make me come?" Felix asked.

"I'm not," Liam assured him. "You're not going to come again until I'm inside you."

Felix knew he'd just been given an order, one he wanted to obey.

Liam led him up the stairs slowly, guiding him up one step at a time. Even though the layout of the house was a mirror image of his own, Felix got all turned around and couldn't figure out if Liam was taking him to the front of the house, where the bigger of the two bedrooms would be, or the back of the house. Maybe Liam had a bedroom *and* a playroom. He thought about asking but decided either Liam would tell him or he'd find out when he was allowed to take the blindfold off.

"Wait here," Liam said, letting him go and moving away from him.

Felix did as he was told, wriggling his toes in the soft, thick carpet. He expected to feel vulnerable without Liam's support, given that he was naked and blindfolded, but he didn't. He felt sexy, and even though he knew he was acting submissively, he felt empowered.

He heard the soft chink of metal as Liam returned to him. Liam stroked something smooth over his skin, and he caught a whiff of leather. He held his breath.

"These are leather cuffs," Liam said. "I'm going to put them around your wrists and ankles."

Felix nodded to give permission. Liam worked gently. The cuffs, though thick and firm, were surprisingly soft against his skin. Next, Liam pressed something hard into his hands, allowing him to explore and feel the long rod of cool metal.

"Do you know what it is?" Liam asked.

"No."

"It's a spreader bar," Liam explained, guiding Felix's

fingers to a pair of clips—like the ones on the end of Domino's leash—in the centre of the bar. "These attach to the rings on the cuffs you're wearing. There's a clip at either end too."

Felix could barely breathe.

"Are you still okay with this?" Liam asked.

All Felix could do was nod. His tongue felt heavy in his mouth, and he was practically drooling as his mind tried to figure out how Liam was going to bind him.

"Legs shoulder-width apart," Liam ordered. "Bend over and hold your ankles with your hands."

If Felix hadn't done yoga most mornings, he would have probably found the position harder to balance in blindfolded than he did.

"I'm going to bind you now," Liam told him. "Then I'm going to spank you. Then, while your arse is still bright red, I'm going to fuck you."

Felix quivered with excitement. He stayed where he was, clutching his ankles just above the cuffs, waiting for orders from Liam.

Liam's hand ran down Felix's leg, thigh to ankle. There was the soft chink of a clip being attached to a ring. Using his foot, Liam nudged Felix's legs apart a little more so his feet were planted slightly wider than the width of his shoulders. There was another chink, and Felix could feel the unyielding hardness of the spreader bar between his ankles, forbidding him from moving his legs closer together or farther apart. Next, Liam took Felix's hand away from his ankle, bringing his wrist to what felt like the centre of the bar. Another chink and Felix could only move his wrist a millimetre or two; the ring and clip jangled against each other as he tried. Liam did the same with his other arm, completely immobilising him.

Felix knew how submissive he had to look, face down, arse up, effectively presenting himself to be spanked or fucked or whatever else Liam decided to do to him. He was completely vulnerable, yet all he could feel was excitement building within him.

He realised the silent pause was to give him time to decide if he was happy to go on.

"Green," he said. "I'm okay, Daddy."

"Good boy. I'm going to take my clothes off now."

Sure enough, Felix heard the clunk of Liam's belt as it landed somewhere close by. All he could do was imagine Liam taking off his jeans, socks, and T-shirt and adding them to the pile that had started with his belt. It was easy to conjure up a visual image of his lover's naked body, as he'd seen plenty of it the day before. Not being able to see Liam added to how titillating the whole experience was.

The floorboards squeaked and moved slightly as Liam walked behind him. Felix held his breath as he felt Liam's leg, covered in thick hair, brush against his own. Then there was space between them again.

Felix knew he was going to be spanked, but without being able to see what Liam was doing, he had no warning before Liam's hand came down on his arse. Perhaps a dozen blows rained down upon him hard and fast. Felix couldn't keep count. He was disorientated and flitting between shock and pleasure so quickly he was left feeling dizzy. His body swayed, and he was sure he was going to fall arse over head, but then Liam's strong hands held his hips, steadying him while he caught his breath.

"Are you okay, boy?" Liam asked.

"Yes, Daddy." Felix licked his lips.

A pang of loss twisted his gut when Liam moved away from him again, but he returned seconds later. The pop of a cap excited him. He shivered violently when cold lube was drizzled down his arse crack, but he didn't have time to complain before Liam's fingers were teasing him. He began to sway again as his legs shook. He wasn't sure if it was because his body was getting tired from the position he was bound in—his muscles *were* aching—or if it was from excitement at what was going to happen next. Liam steadied him with one hand again while his other kept stimulating his arsehole.

"Is my bum red, Daddy?" he asked.

"Yes," Liam said. "Such a beautiful, bright shade."

Felix groaned as Liam pushed what felt like two fingers inside him. His lover slowly pumped them in and out, pressing gently against Felix's prostate every time.

"Oh, Daddy," Felix moaned.

The blindfold… Being bound… The way Liam was fingering him… It was a heady combination that left his cock throbbing with the need to release.

"Daddy," he whined. "Please!"

"You're not ready yet, boy," Liam told him.

Felix felt ready, but he wasn't going to argue. He let himself drift on the wave of his enjoyment, feeling weightless, knowing that Liam would keep him on his feet.

He had no idea how long Liam fingered him. He might have added one or even two more fingers at some point. It was hard to tell. All Felix knew was that he was eager for Liam's cock. Aching for it. He sobbed when Liam's fingers left him, and then shivered when his Daddy trailed damp fingers over his arse.

"Condom," Liam said. "Can you stand on your own?"

"I think so."

Somehow, he found the strength and balance to stay upright while a wrapper rustled behind him. The next sensation he felt was Liam's wet, slick cock sliding back and forth along his arse crack.

"Oh, Daddy," he whimpered. "I need you."

Liam entered him slowly and gently. His cock was so thick and long, but Felix knew he could take it, and fuck, did he need to take it.

"I'm going to fuck you hard," Liam said. "Let me know if it's not good for you."

Felix nodded. His heart fluttered, and as much as he wanted Liam, he couldn't help but feel a twist of fear in his gut. He'd been fucked roughly before, but not by anyone as big as Liam, but he knew his Daddy would take care of him, so the fear fluttered away like a dandelion seed caught on a breeze. Even so, he yelped with surprise when Liam hammered his hips back and forth, harder than he'd expected. But as soon as the shock passed, his body hummed. He was caught even more off guard when Liam began to slap his arse again. Not as hard as before but enough that he could feel it. Each slap was perfectly timed with a hard forward thrust of Liam's hips. Within seconds, Felix was delirious from the mix of pleasure and pain. His body trembled and shook as he tried, and failed, to hold his orgasm back until he was given permission to come. Liam drove into him faster and spanked him harder. Slaps and groans filled the air. Felix's arse stung in more ways than one, but oh God, it felt so good.

"Daddy!" he cried as he felt his balls draw up tight again. Surely, he couldn't be ready to have another orgasm? Maybe Liam had been jackhammering into him for longer than he'd realised. "Daddy!"

He felt the wave of a second orgasm hit him. Liam shuddered behind him and in him, thrusting hard and long as he came. They both breathed harshly, and Felix's body was coated with sweat. From what little he could feel of Liam, he knew his lover's was too.

Almost reverently, Liam withdrew and unclipped Felix from the spacer bar, helping him to stand tall. He removed the cuffs, kissing each of Felix's bared wrists and ankles as he did so. Finally, he removed the blindfold and stared into Felix's eyes. All Felix could do was collapse forward into his Daddy's arms, exhausted and spent.

23

LIAM

"Was that good for you, boy?" Liam asked as he held Felix.

Felix nodded against his chest. "I hope it was good for you too?"

Liam kissed his boy's hair. "So, so good. Thank you for letting me play with you."

He led Felix to the bed that was in the room, and they snuggled up together under the quilt. They were in the spare room, overlooking the garden. Until that evening his toys had been stored in labelled packing boxes, which he'd almost thrown out several times. It wasn't like he'd had a boy since he'd moved into the house or for some time before that, but with Felix lying in his arms, he was glad he'd kept them.

"Wait here," he whispered.

"I'm not going anywhere," Felix murmured sleepily. "Don't be long."

"I won't be."

Liam retrieved some lotion from the bathroom.

"Lie on your stomach," he ordered when he returned.

Felix grumbled a bit but turned off his side, so he was lying flat on his stomach, resting his cheek on his folded arms. Liam began to massage the lotion into Felix's bright red arse to soothe it.

"That's nice," Felix said.

"Less sore?"

"Not yet. I think you need to keep doing that for a lot longer to make it all better."

Liam smiled. He loved Felix's sassiness. For all that he grumbled and complained about how annoying Felix was, he loved everything about the young man.

"Stay the night?"

Felix's brow tugged into a frown. "I can't leave Domino alone that long. Stay at mine?"

"You could bring him over here?" Liam suggested, even though he was probably going to regret having a young dog in the house. Was he even fully house-trained yet? "He needs to get used to the place before he stays here on his own." He wasn't sure Felix had taken him seriously when he'd offered to look after the puppy while he travelled to the States for his audition.

Felix smiled. "That's a good idea. I'll bring his bed. Except—" He giggled. "My shorts are kind of wrecked. I can't exactly nip home naked."

"You can borrow my dressing gown."

"Thank you."

"And you can pick up clothes for tomorrow," Liam suggested. "Along with whatever you wear in bed." He hadn't forgotten the question that Felix had refused to answer.

Felix laughed. "I don't wear anything in bed." He pushed up to kiss Liam. "*Ever.*"

Liam generally at least wore pyjama bottoms, but he was more than happy to forget to put them on so he could be naked next to Felix.

"Would you tell me about your time as a detective?" Felix asked. "And why you left?"

Liam sighed. He should have known that Felix would want to dig deeper after the little he'd told him during the ridiculous game he'd been forced to play.

"There's not much to tell."

"It must have been a fascinating job," Felix pressed.

"It was. Fascinating. Demanding. Soul-destroying." Liam stared up at the ceiling rather than at the beautiful young man beside him. "I realised just how dark the world was and that people are capable of the most horrific things."

"Not everyone," Felix said softly. "Not even most people. Just a few."

Liam pinched the bridge of his nose. "I thought like that for the first few years, but the longer I did the job... The more cases I investigated... The more I saw the terrible things that people would do to each other— to strangers, to people they were meant to love, to *children*—I lost all the faith I'd ever had in humanity. In the end, I couldn't take it anymore. I couldn't deal with people anymore. I took early retirement and bought this place."

"You've been hiding from the world," Felix said sadly.

"I wouldn't say that exactly," Liam huffed.

"I would." Felix stroked Liam's arm. "I get it. I really do. You've seen a lot of terrible things. I'm sure there are cases that you still carry with you, even now."

Liam sucked in a shuddering breath. Wasn't that the truth?

"But hiding from the world won't make the pain of those cases go away," Felix pointed out. "You might be trying to avoid everything ugly about the world, but you're also missing out on everything beautiful."

Liam knew Felix was right, but it hadn't bothered him until recently. He'd been fine in his quiet little bubble, with nothing but himself and his roses to worry about. Then Felix had bounded into his life and upended everything. His beautiful boy, sunshine personified, had given him someone else to care about. His only worry was that he cared too much.

"We should go and get the puppy," he said.

"Are you changing the subject, Daddy?" Felix asked accusingly. A smile quirked his lips up.

"Yes."

Felix squeezed his arm. "I know you can't tell me anything specific, but you *can* talk to me. I know I don't always come across as very mature or sensible, but I can be when I need to be. I'm here, Liam. Whatever hurt you've been carrying around all this time, you don't need to carry it alone anymore."

Liam's heart squeezed tight. Tears stung his eyes, though none fell. He dragged Felix onto his lap, kissing his lips, jaw, and neck, too overwhelmed with gratitude to speak. Knowing that Felix wanted to share his emotional burdens, even though he couldn't, was overwhelming.

"Thank you," he managed. His throat felt thick with emotions.

"I can take care of you too, Daddy," Felix said, resting his forehead against Liam's. He stroked his fingers through Liam's beard. "I want to."

"As long as it doesn't involve cooking for me?"

Felix laughed loudly. "I still say making pizza counts as cooking."

Liam rolled his eyes. "You would." He patted Felix's arse. "Let's go and get Domino, and then we can settle down for the night. In my bedroom," he added in case Felix was wondering.

Felix glanced around. "This doesn't *look* like a playroom."

"You've been in lots, have you?"

Felix smiled sheepishly. "Only in clubs."

"It's not a playroom," Liam confirmed. "But we could turn it into one if you like. It's not as if anyone ever stays here."

Felix frowned. "You don't have any family?"

"There's my sister and her family. They visit for the day occasionally, and I visit them. There's no room for them all to stay here, though. So..." He ran his thumb down Felix's cheek. "Do you want a room we can play in?"

Felix bit his lip. "I think you'd need to put a lock on the door so your nieces and nephews don't wander in."

Liam chuckled. "That could be arranged."

"I wouldn't know where to start with what we'd have in here," Felix admitted.

"I do. We can talk about the kinds of things we both want to do and look at equipment together. If you want," he added. As excited as he was by the thought, he didn't want to make Felix feel like he was under any pressure.

"I do want to," Felix said, his eyes bright and eager. "But you'll have to guide me."

"I can do that." He kissed the boy tenderly. "Let's get your dog."

Leaving Felix for a few minutes, he went to his bedroom to pull on some jogging bottoms and a T-shirt before taking his dressing gown back to Felix.

They entered Felix's house a few minutes later to the sound of a phone ringing. Not that Felix made any attempt to find the phone, calling the puppy's name instead.

"Shouldn't you get that?" Liam asked as Domino came racing out of the kitchen, colliding with Felix's legs.

"Crazy puppy," Felix said, crouching to give the dog lots of fuss. "Nah, it's probably just Emma. She's a few hours behind us."

"Your agent?"

"Yes."

A chill crept into Liam's gut. "Will it be about your audition?"

Felix shrugged. "Probably."

"You should answer it, then."

Felix looked up, cracking a smile. "It's not ringing anymore. She can call back tomorrow."

Ignoring Felix's wish, the phone started to ring again.

"Answer it," Liam urged. "I can wait."

Felix pouted but wandered off into the kitchen anyway. The phone stopped ringing, and then Liam heard the muffled sound of Felix as he talked to whoever was on the other end of the line.

Sitting at his feet, Domino whined at him, eyes huge and pleading.

"Go on, then," he muttered, bending over to give the puppy a quick pat.

The dog wagged its tail crazily, panting in excitement.

"You want more?" Liam asked.

He wasn't going to get anything done while the damn creature was staying with him. He hoped Felix wouldn't be gone for long. He sat cross-legged on the floor, giving the puppy more of a fuss.

"Oh no, get away with you," he growled as the dog crawled into his lap.

Domino ignored him and settled down, head resting on his paws.

"Damn dog."

"He likes you." Felix chuckled from the doorway to the kitchen. He was leaning against the door jamb, arms loosely folded.

"He's a pest."

"But he's cute," Felix said. "Don't you think he's cute?"

"A cute pest," Liam grumbled. "Was it your agent?"

"Yeah."

"And?"

"I've got an audition next Thursday. She's booked me a flight out on Wednesday and one home on Saturday, though there's a crazy layover, so I won't get back until Sunday."

Felix would be going in five days, for five days. Why did five days feel both too short and too long at the same time?

"She's very excited," Felix went on. "If I get it, she thinks it's going to be the film that catapults me into the big leagues." He dipped his chin.

"You're nervous?"

Felix nodded. "I'm always nervous before auditions, but I hadn't realised quite how big a deal this film was. It's with one of the top directors in Hollywood. It's got a *huge* budget, and one of the other leads has already been cast. I… I can't tell you who it is, but she's massive. One of the top-paid actresses in the world, and I'd be auditioning to play her son. If I get the role…" He shook his head as though not quite believing it. "Emma reckons it's an Oscar fodder movie."

It was weird to see Felix so worried and so animated. Excitement rang clear in his voice; his eyes were bright and shining. Yet every word felt like a punch in the gut to Liam. If Felix got this role, he wouldn't hang around in a house at the edge of a sleepy seaside village. He'd be too busy with parties, award ceremonies, and TV opportunities.

"It would be more money than I've ever earned

before," Felix went on. "Emma thinks I'll be able to pick and choose films after this rather than having to audition. *If* I get it," he repeated as though reminding himself to keep his feet on the ground.

"You *will* get it," Liam said, even though it hurt to say the words.

Felix laughed. "You don't watch films, let alone *my* films. For all you know, I'm the most wooden actor that ever lived."

"You wouldn't have been acting for seventeen years if that was true," Liam pointed out.

"I don't know about that."

Liam dislodged the puppy from his lap and stood so he could go to Felix and gently grasp his shoulders. "You deserve this chance, Felix. Go to the audition."

Felix stared up into his eyes, as though he were searching for something. "Is that what you want me to do?" he asked finally.

Liam smiled, though he wondered if he looked sad rather than supportive; he hoped not. "Is it what *you* want. Do *you* want the role? That's all that matters."

Felix nodded hesitantly. "Yes... I think so... I mean... I've worked hard for a long time to get an opportunity like this."

"Then don't let it slip through your fingers," Liam said.

He pulled Felix close, kissing his boy's head. He had to force himself to swallow the bitter truth that he'd fallen for a boy who was destined for a bright future. One that was too bright to be traded in for the quiet life that Liam could offer him.

24

FELIX

Emma had made all the travel arrangements, so there wasn't much for Felix to do over the next few days, except learn the audition script, perfect his accent, and spend as much time with Liam and Domino as he could. He'd managed to arrange for the decorators to come into the house while he was away to get everything done. Hopefully, it wouldn't smell too badly of paint when he got back. If it did, he was fairly confident he could persuade Liam to let him stay over for a few nights, and Domino, of course. Even though Liam hadn't admitted it out loud, it was obvious he was falling for the puppy too.

He'd sensed a little sadness in Liam over the last couple of days and had decided it was his duty to cheer his lover up. After some quick searching on the internet, he'd found the perfect way to do it. *Two* perfect ways, in fact. He was confident Liam would love one of gifts, but wasn't so sure about the other. There was a very real chance that Liam would hate it and spank him for being so ridiculous, but he knew he was going to have one hell of an afternoon either way.

He stood on the bench so he could see into Liam's garden more easily. As usual, his lover was looking after his roses.

"Hey, neighbour," Felix said cheerfully.

Liam left the roses to come to the fence. He put his hand on the back of Felix's neck, pulling him down for a hot kiss.

"Are you trying to get in my pants?" Felix asked playfully.

"Always," Liam said in a gravelly tone. "Have you practised your lines today?"

"Not yet."

Liam gave him a disapproving look.

"It's fine. I know them. I've got some presents for you."

"Presents?" Liam's eyebrows lifted.

"To remember me by." Felix pursed his lips. "Actually, one of them is for me to remember *you* by, but I'm sure you'll appreciate it too."

"You make it sound like you're going away for months, not five days." Liam's voice was heavy and stiff.

"Five days is a long time. Without me, you're going to go back to your old grumpy ways."

Liam rolled his eyes.

Felix ducked down to retrieve the first gift, a young rose bush in a planting bag. He lifted it over the fence to Liam.

"All the roses you've told me about are named after people," Felix explained as Liam looked at the pretty yellow rose heads. "I couldn't find a rose called Felix, but I decided this one would do." He turned the information label so Liam could see it.

"You are my sunshine," Liam read.

"Aww, thank you!"

Liam snorted.

"Do you like it?"

"It's nice," Liam said gruffly.

Felix grinned, knowing he'd made a good choice. He retrieved the second gift, which he'd removed from the discreet packaging it had been shipped in.

"Do you want your second present?"

Liam pinched his lips together, barely nodding. Felix presented the gift to him, laughing uncontrollably as Liam's jaw dropped and his eyes widened in horror. Felix was holding a long, wide tube, which was black with a luminous blue cock emblazoned on the side, with the words 'Clone-A-Cock' printed in bold black lettering.

"You're not serious," Liam said flatly. "This is a joke."

"Nope," Felix said between giggles. "You did say you didn't want anything else inside me but you, so I thought I'd better have a version of your cock that I can take with me."

Liam shook his head and stalked away, cradling the rose. Still laughing, Felix left his own garden and let himself into Liam's.

"Come on, grumpy bear," he said, following Liam like a shadow as his lover gathered the things he'd need to plant the new rose bush. "You like the idea, really."

"No, I don't."

"It'll be fun," Felix said in a drawn-out sing-song tone.

"No, it won't."

"Please?"

"It's ridiculous. *You're* ridiculous."

"So you keep telling me. But you love me, really."

Liam grumbled something under his breath. "Why the fuck is it *blue*?" he asked in a huffy tone.

"It glows in the dark. I *could* have got a skin-coloured one, but what would have been the fun in that?"

Liam turned around and glared at him. "It's not fun. It looks downright dangerous. I'm not sticking my cock in… In…"

"I'm guessing it's some kind of plaster," Felix said with a shrug. "It's got to be safe, or they wouldn't be allowed to sell the kits."

Liam shook his head. "Forget it. Send it back."

Felix put on his best pout and puppy dog eyes. "Please, Daddy? I was thinking of you when I bought it."

"I don't see that I'm going to get anything out of it."

"That's not true. I'll help you get hard so we can make the mould, and then I'll help you deal with your hard-on afterwards. It'll be fun." He pushed close to Liam, rubbing his body against his lover's. "Naughty, sexy, fun."

"I should spank you for suggesting something so stupid," Liam grumbled.

"Mmm, yes, please!"

Liam blew out a disapproving breath before stalking away to one of the raised rose beds that actually had some space in it. He knelt and started to dig a hole for the new rose.

"You're being mean," Felix taunted.

"How?"

"First you won't let me clone your cock." He couldn't actually say it without snorting with laughter. "Then, you as good as promise me a spanking but don't deliver. Maybe *I* should be the one punishing *you*."

"You're not going to let this go, are you?"

"Nope."

"Even if I try to spank the ridiculous notion out of you?"

"Admit it. You want me to clone your cock." Felix chuckled over the words again. "You like the idea that I'll be fucking myself with a perfect copy of it while I'm away."

What he wouldn't have given to have been able to see into his lover's mind in that instant to find out exactly what thoughts were running through it.

"I'd be very grateful," he added. "If I'm happy, you'd be happy, but if you make me sad…"

"Fine," Liam grated out through clenched teeth. "Just let me plant the rose first."

Felix bent down to kiss Liam's cheek. "I'll go get things ready. Don't go chickening out on me!"

He skipped inside and emptied the contents of the tube onto the worktop, studying the instructions while he waited for Liam to join him.

Liam took his sweet time. When he eventually came

into the kitchen, his hands were filthy from working with the soil.

"It's planted," he said. "Thank you for the rose. It was a nice thought."

"You're welcome."

Liam washed his hands and then looked at the items that Felix had arranged. "You really are serious, aren't you?"

"Yup."

"Dear God, help me."

"The only person who's going to help you is me."

"How so?"

"Well, you've got to get hard to make the mould. You don't think I'll leave you all frustrated afterwards, do you?"

"Let's get this over with," Liam snapped. "And if I end up in hospital—"

Felix laughed. "You're *not* going to end up in hospital. It's perfectly safe. Get your cock out." Felix held up the clear plastic tube that had contained everything. "We've got to cut this to the right size. I could guess, but I wouldn't want to waste it by underestimating how big you are."

Still grumbling, Liam undid his jeans and pushed them down enough to free his flaccid cock from his underwear.

"You need to be hard," Felix said playfully. "Want me to help?"

"Down on your knees."

"Yes, Daddy."

Felix knelt and wrapped his hand around the base of

Liam's cock. He knew he didn't have enough control of his gag reflex to take the whole of Liam's length into his mouth, so he used his hand to stroke up and down as he licked the head of Liam's cock, swirling his tongue in varying patterns. He had to stretch his lips to get them around the mushroom head. Even that filled his mouth. He stared up at Liam as he sucked and licked, glad his lover wasn't thrusting deeper into his mouth like so many guys did. It didn't take him long to get Liam's cock hard, but he pleasured his lover for a little longer, enjoying watching the way Liam's eyelashes fluttered, as he listened to the moans of pleasure that poured out of his mouth.

"I think you're ready," he said, wiping the mixture of saliva and pre-cum from his lips with the back of his hand.

He grabbed the clear tube from the counter and placed it over Liam's cock until the edge of the tube was pressed against his body.

"It has to be one inch longer," Felix said, amused that he wasn't going to have to cut that much off the length of the tube. "Why don't you keep yourself hard while I make it the right length?"

"I'll do it. You can keep me hard."

Felix waggled his eyebrows. "I knew you'd enjoy it."

"I'm enjoying your mouth on my cock, nothing else," Liam snapped, grabbing the tube from Felix's hands.

"You'll need to put tape around the edge once you've cut it," Felix said. "And then mix the plaster."

"I can read instructions. Now, suck."

Felix licked his lips and then got back to work with his hand and mouth as he watched Liam cut the tube and put tape around it. Next, Liam picked up the instructions and read them. Felix wasn't sure how his lover was concentrating. *He* wouldn't have been able to read instructions while Liam was giving him a blow job.

"It looks like cocaine," Liam grumbled as he investigated the big bag of white powder. "It says here it needs to be mixed with water at thirty-two degrees."

Very precise, but the temperature made sense. It would be slightly above body temperature, making it pleasantly hot, like the water in a jacuzzi. Thinking of which, Felix definitely had to get a jacuzzi in the garden. Bubbly sex with Liam was high up on his to-do list.

"Stop," Liam said in an irritated tone.

Felix obeyed.

"I need to get the water."

Felix waited on his knees for Liam to run the tap water and get it to the right temperature. Liam brought the water, in a bowl, back to the spot he'd been standing in. He motioned to Felix to carry on while he opened the bag of powder.

"You've got to stir for exactly sixty seconds," Felix warned.

"I know what I'm doing."

Felix chuckled and resumed his pleasurable task. Liam used his watch to time himself as he mixed the powder into the water. When the minute was done, he poured the mixture into the tube. It looked pretty gross, all thick and gloopy.

"You're seriously expecting me to put my cock in there?" Liam asked, grimacing.

"Yes!"

"You're going to owe me for this."

"I can cope with that."

Felix helped Liam to put his cock into the tube, giggling as some of the mixture dripped out when it was displaced.

"It feels like porridge," Liam complained.

"You make a habit of sticking your cock in porridge, do you?" Felix asked innocently, grabbing a cloth to clean up the drips.

Liam glared at him.

"Hey, each to their own. I'm not going to judge you for being kinky enough to fuck a bowl of porridge."

"I'm going to spank you," Liam threatened.

"Your hands are a little occupied at the moment."

"How long do I have to keep this awful thing on?" Liam asked.

"I thought you'd read the instructions?"

Liam narrowed his eyes. "How long?"

"One or two minutes. Let me help you pass the time." Felix stood and began to run his fingers through Liam's beard, pushing up onto his tiptoes so he could kiss his lover.

"Get this thing off me," Liam grumbled when the kiss ended.

Felix helped him to remove the tube carefully.

"What now?" Liam asked.

"We have to leave it for four hours, so…" Felix wrapped his hand around Liam's cock. "Now, we play?"

It was pretty easy to fill the four hours while they waited for the mould to cool down and set. Not that they were timing it accurately, so Felix was pretty sure they'd gone over. After showering, they went back downstairs to finish making the dildo, Liam grumbling all the way.

Felix checked over the instructions again.

"We've got to mix the two jars of silicone for at least two minutes."

He began pouring them into the disposable container that had been provided in the kit, making sure to get all the mixture out before stirring it.

"This was more fun when you were sucking my cock," Liam complained. "Oh God, that looks disgusting!"

The gloopy bright blue mixture did look pretty gross.

"Are you really going to put that up your arse?"

"Not until its set!" Felix cackled. "I knew this was going to be fun, but you're making it funnier than I expected."

He poured it carefully into the mould. "Right, we need to put the vibrator through a piece of cardboard to stop it falling in and then push it into the silicone."

Liam found a piece of cardboard and some scissors. After making a small cross in the cardboard and pushing the vibrator through, Felix squished it into the silicone mix. Some of it oozed out of the top, which only made Liam grumble even more about how disgusting it was. Felix laughed as he cleaned up the mess.

"*Now* how long do we have to leave it?"

"Twenty-four hours."

Liam put his hands on Felix's hips and pulled him close. "Just in time for you to take with you."

Felix grinned. "That *was* the idea. Thank you for indulging me."

Liam wrinkled his nose. "It's a good thing I like you."

"Oh, so you *do* like me? I knew you'd admit it eventually."

"I do," Liam said, his deep voice purring out of him. "I like you a lot."

LIAM

The taxi pulled up outside at some ungodly hour in the morning. They were already awake. Liam wasn't sure Felix had slept at all, as he'd been so hyperactive. Even the puppy was awake and whining as he stared at Felix's carry-on suitcase, which was all he was taking with him. The boy was definitely travelling light.

"I could come with you to the airport," Liam said, placing his hands on either side of Felix's face.

"I'd love you to, but—"

"I know." Liam sighed.

They'd talked about it already. The airport was a long way away. If Liam went with Felix, he'd be away for several hours—too long to leave Domino alone. It still made Liam's chest ache that this was goodbye.

He'd tried to tell himself it was a temporary parting. Five days and Felix would bounce back into his life, as happy and annoying as ever. But he knew that wasn't true. Felix was about to go back to the life he'd left behind. Although Liam hadn't asked Felix for details, he'd got the impression that his movie lifestyle was fast-paced and full of parties and clubs. He'd go back to that and realise he wanted it far more than a quiet life in the British countryside. Liam had to face facts. They wanted different things out of life. They might have had a few amazing days together, but ultimately, they weren't compatible.

He picked up the puppy to make sure it didn't try to chase Felix out the door. It also gave him something else to focus on other than the goodbye. Something else to hold other than his boy.

Felix messed with Domino's floppy ears. "You take care of him," he said before looking up at Liam and grinning.

"I don't need taking care of," Liam huffed.

"Sure you do, grumpy bear. Who else is going to keep you on your toes while I'm gone?"

A horn beeped outside.

"I'd better go before he drives off without me." Felix sighed. "I'm going to miss you, Daddy."

"Call me."

"As soon as I can."

Felix ran his fingers through Liam's beard, stroked Domino, and then went to the door where he paused.

"Bye, neighbour."

"Bye, boy." A lump formed in Liam's throat.

Felix opened the door.

"Felix."

He looked back, eyebrows lifted as he met Liam's stare.

Liam cleared his throat. "I really like you."

A grin lit up Felix's face. "I really like you too, grumpy bear." He pressed his palm to his lips and blew Liam a dramatic kiss.

Liam rolled his eyes.

"Look on the bright side," Felix said. "Your eye muscles will get a break while I'm not here." He winked at Liam and then slipped out the door, closing it firmly behind him before Liam could drag him back for a good spanking.

Seconds later, the taxi door thumped shut, and the engine rumbled as the car pulled away. Domino whimpered, and Liam felt like doing the same.

"It's only for a few days," he told the puppy as he carried him through to the kitchen. He opened the back door and let the puppy out into the garden.

The house already felt too empty and too quiet.

He waited for Domino to toilet before bringing him back inside and then tried to settle the puppy in his bed, which he'd put in the kitchen, but the tiny furball kept whining and following him every time he tried to leave the room.

"Fine," he grumbled.

He had been planning on trying to get some more sleep upstairs in his comfortable bed. Instead, he let the puppy follow him into the sitting room. He lay down on the sofa. The puppy sat on its haunches and stared at him.

"What? You can sleep on the floor."

The puppy looked at him with big, sad eyes.

"You're as annoying as your owner, do you know that?"

The puppy whined.

"Are you even allowed on the sofa?"

Domino cocked his head to one side. Liam didn't need the puppy to be able to answer the question. He'd seen the puppy curled up with Felix on the sofa next door a few days earlier. He patted the sofa, inviting the dog to join him.

Domino jumped up and immediately settled down with his front paws and head resting on Liam's chest. He continued to stare at Liam with big, sad eyes, almost like a manifestation of his own feelings of loss.

"Good God," he muttered to the puppy. "We're both acting like lovesick teenagers. He'll be back in five days. Stop being pathetic."

He closed his eyes and tried to settle into sleep, but his mind provided him with a rerun of the steamy night he'd spent with Felix instead. How the boy hadn't been exhausted enough to sleep after they'd finished, Liam didn't know. Clearly pre-audition excitement trumped post-orgasmic tiredness.

He dozed with the puppy for a short while and then got too frustrated with not sleeping to stay put any longer. He was determined to fill his days as he'd done before Felix had moved in next door, but as he went through the motions, he found himself missing his boy more and more. There was no ridiculously loud yoga music to annoy him. Felix wasn't in the garden in his absurd yoga shorts. He really was being pathetic.

He was halfway through breakfast when he received a text from Felix.

—At the airport and through security. Your cock received some raised eyebrows.

Liam almost choked on his cereal.

—You took it out of your suitcase?

—I had to, grumpy bear. It's an electronic device ;-)

Liam felt like dying on the spot. He should have never allowed Felix to make a mould of his cock.

—I'll think of you when I use it, after I land. I'll need something to keep me from getting all jittery about my audition.

How could Liam stay embarrassed or annoyed with *that* image firmly planted in his mind? He wished he could watch Felix pleasuring himself with the dildo, but hotel WI-FI wouldn't be secure enough—or strong enough—for a sexy live stream. He made a mental note to ask Felix if he could watch him use it when he got home.

Another text from Felix lit up his phone.

—I'm bored.

Liam smiled.

—Already? You've only just got there.

—I know, and I've got over an hour before my flight takes off. Entertain me, neighbour.

—How?

—I don't know. Send me dick pics or something.

Liam chuckled.

—Can't you just look in your suitcase?

—It's not the same. Damn, there's not a pouty face emoticon.

"Domino," Liam called.

The puppy scampered to him and sat, looking up at him expectantly.

"Felix wants a photo."

Domino wagged his tail as Liam took a photo and sent it to Felix.

—*That's not a dick pic. Give Domino big squishy hugs for me.*

Liam was *not* going to give the puppy 'big squishy hugs'. He did give him a quick stroke.

—*Bored.*

Liam decided to ignore the text while he finished his breakfast.

—*Bored.*

Liam began to wash up.

—*Still bored.*

He cleaned the bowl and his coffee mug and set them on the side.

—*Where's my dick pic?*

He dried his hands and picked up the phone, dialling Felix's number.

"I'm not going to send you a dick pic," he said when Felix answered.

"*Please?*"

"No."

"You're no fun."

"I *did* offer to come with you to the airport."

"You wouldn't have been able to come through security with me," Felix said sullenly. "So I'd still be bored."

"How are you going to cope with a thirteen-hour flight?"

"I've got an hour in the airport in Amsterdam. I'm

not actually going to spend thirteen hours on a plane. But I could watch movies, I guess." He yawned. "Maybe try and get some sleep?"

"You need to sleep," Liam agreed. "I don't think you slept at all last night."

"Did I keep you awake?" There was concern in Felix's voice.

"Not all the time. I can nap during the day to catch up if your damn dog will let me."

"Aww, does he miss me?" Felix asked.

"Yes."

Liam's chest tightened. "When's your audition?"

"Just before lunch tomorrow, which gives me a bit of time to chill after I land."

There was a pause. In the background, Liam could hear tinny announcements and the hum of people talking. There was also the clatter of dishes, suggesting that Felix was in one of the many airport eateries.

"Emma's got some things lined up for me while I'm there," Felix picked up. "A couple of meals with casting directors for different projects and a radio interview, so from tomorrow it'll be all go until I'm on my way home."

It felt good to hear Felix refer to the UK as 'home', but Liam didn't allow any hope to build up inside him.

"How's my rose?" Felix asked.

"It's *my* rose," Liam reminded him.

Felix chuckled. "You know what I mean."

Liam glanced out into the garden. The rose Felix had given him was easy to see. The strong morning sunshine made its yellow leaves look bright and cheerful, just like Felix. It was the best present Felix could have given him.

"It's fine."

He hoped he'd been careful enough that he hadn't damaged the root system when he'd planted it, but only time would tell. He realised the background noise had changed. Felix had moved somewhere quieter.

"Can I be really needy for a sec?" Felix asked.

"Yes," Liam said. Not that Felix would have listened if he'd said 'no'.

"I'm missing you already, Daddy," Felix whispered.

Was it wrong that those words made Liam feel happy?

"You'll be home in a few days. You won't have time to think about me with all the partying you'll be doing."

Felix chuckled. "I'll be going to parties, will I?"

"Yes. Lots of them."

"And clubs?"

"Almost certainly."

"Kinky clubs?"

"No!" Liam hadn't meant to snap.

"I wasn't being serious." He heard Felix suck in a breath. "I won't let anyone but you lay a hand on me, Daddy."

Liam breathed a sigh of relief. Despite all the uncertainty around their future together, it had been good to hear Felix say those words.

26

FELIX

Too many hours of breathing recycled air on the plane had left Felix with a tickle in the back of his throat and a mild headache. He stretched and yawned as he stood in line for passport control, glad to be able to move properly again—wandering up and down the central aisle of the plane did not count. Sadly, although he had been recognised by a few people, including staff, it hadn't been enough to get him bumped up to business or first class.

He smiled to himself as he thought about how uncomfortable Liam would be on a plane, with his knees jammed up to his chest, having to confine his muscly bulk in a too-narrow space. He'd probably hate it.

Felix turned his phone on as soon as he cleared passport control. It took a few minutes to find a new network and connect to it, during which time he'd bypassed baggage pickup and was on his way out of the terminal. His phone beeped as it received a delayed message.

—*I hope you had a good flight.*

It was probably crazy that a caring text from Liam left him grinning from ear to ear, but he wasn't about to second guess his reaction. Liam made him happy. Simple.

"Felix!"

It didn't take him long to spot Emma. She was holding a card with his first name on it. Not that she needed to. She looked a lot fresher than he felt, and was perfectly put together, as always. She'd cut her hair into an off-the-shoulder bob and coloured it ash blonde, although darker roots were just starting to show.

"How was the flight?" she asked as he joined her.

"Long."

"I'll take you to the hotel so you can freshen up," she said as she led him out of the busy airport towards the short-term car park. "I've got a meeting set up for you this afternoon to discuss your radio interview on Friday morning. There's a film premiere tonight that you need to be seen at and what promises to be an amazing party after. Again, getting your face in front of the camera would be a good thing."

Felix stared at her, bewildered. He'd been looking forward to some R and R for the rest of the day so he would be fresh for the audition.

"Why do I need to show my face?"

Emma glanced at him, rolling her eyes even harder than Liam normally did. "To keep yourself current,

Felix. You need to stay in people's minds if you want to be considered for bigger roles."

He shook his head. "I had a film out what, three months ago? It's been less than a month since my face was splashed on the front cover of a magazine."

"That was in the UK," Emma reminded him. "You're bigger there because you're a local star, but you're virtual nobody here, *and* it's been a while since you did a magazine spread or a talk show spot." Her eyes lit up as though she was planning something. She probably was.

"It wasn't that long ago," Felix grumbled under his breath as he recalled the gruelling schedule she'd arranged for him around the release of his last film.

Emma stopped and turned around so suddenly that he almost crashed into her. "What's the matter?" she demanded.

"I'm tired. It was a long flight. I wasn't expecting to be doing anything this afternoon other than catching up on sleep."

She shook her head. "No sleeping for you until a normal bedtime. It's the fastest way to adjust to jetlag."

"How will I get to bed at a sensible hour if I'm at a party?"

"You'll have fun and forget to be tired once you get there." Emma turned and marched off, leaving him to follow her.

He only half listened to Emma as she filled him in on everything they'd be doing during his short visit, as she drove him to the hotel. He was itching to call Liam but knew Emma would effectively be his shadow for the next several hours, so he contented himself with sending a quick text.

—*Arrived safely. Emma picked me up. She has plans.*

He tried to calculate what time it would be in the UK, but he'd always sucked at time zones, even more so when he had brain fog from tiredness.

—*Plans?*

—*Yeah. Meeting. Film. Party.*

—*All today?*

Felix could almost feel Liam's concern through the simple question.

—*There's no rest for the wicked ;-)*

—*Take care of yourself.*

"Who are you texting?" Emma asked.

Felix gave her the side-eye. "Who are you, my mum?"

She shrugged, keeping her eyes firmly on the busy road ahead. "Close enough."

"My…"

Felix hesitated. What exactly were he and Liam? Lovers, certainly. Daddy and boy. He chuckled. There was no way he was going to share *that* information with Emma. Were they boyfriends? Would Liam even appreciate being referred to as a boyfriend? Partners sounded more grown-up but also one hell of a lot more serious. Too serious?

"Felix?"

"Sorry, I'm tired," Felix reiterated, running a hand over his face. "My boyfriend. I'm texting with my boyfriend."

Emma glanced at him. "I didn't know you had a boyfriend. Is he photogenic?"

"What? No! I mean, yes, but—" He cut himself off and took a deep breath. "No, Emma. He's is off limits. Hell, my whole love life is off limits."

"You're a star, Felix. *Nothing* is off limits."

"You said a few minutes ago that I was a virtual nobody."

She glared ahead at the road. "*In* America. If you get this movie, you won't be. *Everyone* will know your name and your face. You won't be able to keep your love life a secret then, so you'd better get used to the idea of people knowing who you're seeing."

Felix looked out the window, running a finger back and forth along his lower lip. How would Liam react to being the centre of attention? Felix had never hidden the fact that he was gay. He'd been open and honest about it in interviews. As far as he was concerned, part of being in the limelight was being a good role model. How could he do that if he hid who he was? But there was a difference between being out and proud and letting the press know about his relationship with Liam. He'd been photographed with guys before, but they'd been the kind of men who courted that sort of attention. Men who attended the parties and clubs stars went to. Guys who were trying to get a leg up in acting themselves, who thought that being on the arm of someone higher up the chain would help them. Liam was different.

"Tell me about him," Emma said. "I need to know the details."

As much as Felix wanted to object, he knew she was right. She couldn't manage his career if she didn't know what was going on with him.

"He's my new neighbour."

"Go on," she prompted when he fell silent.

"He's an ex-detective."

"Ex…"

Felix could practically hear the cogs whirring in Emma's brain.

"How old is he?"

Felix shrugged. "Late forties. He took early retirement."

"How old?"

"I didn't ask."

"You… *What?*"

"It didn't seem important. Age is just a number."

Emma shook her head. "You're not *that* naïve, Felix. It might not be important to you, but it *will* be important to the world."

"I don't want anyone else to know, Emma. It doesn't need to come up."

"And how long do you think you can keep this relationship a secret, Felix?"

"I dunno."

"Not long, that's for sure. All it will take is for *one* fan to see the two of you together, take a photo and put it on the internet. Then the paparazzi will descend on the pair of you like vultures. And they *will* make a big deal of the age gap, Felix. Twenty-plus years is a big deal."

Felix ran his thumb over his phone screen. "I hadn't even thought about that," he whispered.

No, he'd been too caught up in how amazing Liam made him feel to think about anything beyond the bubble of their two houses. Had Liam? If he hadn't, would he run a mile the minute he realised there was a chance his life could be turned into a media circus? Felix's stomach churned, and he felt sick. He wanted to get to the hotel, lock himself in the bathroom, and call Liam to talk the possible nightmare scenario through. But at the same time, he didn't want to mention it at all.

"Start thinking about it," Emma said. "We can keep this to ourselves for now, but it's going to get out sooner or later, especially if you get this part."

They pulled into the hotel's underground car parking, driving slowly as Emma searched for a spot to park the car.

"You've worked hard for this chance, Felix," she said. "Don't let an affair with an old man put it at risk."

"He's not old. Besides, why would being with Liam put my career at risk?" Felix asked.

"What do you think people are going to say about him?"

Felix shrugged.

"Cradle snatcher comes to mind," Emma said.

"I'm twenty-five."

"Sugar daddy, then. If he was a woman, the press would brand him a cougar."

Felix rubbed at his temples. "Stop," he pleaded. "I wish I hadn't told you."

"I'm glad you did. Is it serious?"

"I think so, yes."

He hadn't spelt out to Liam that he was in love with him, though he was, nor could he speak for Liam. It would take the two of them, working together, to turn what they had into a long-lasting, committed relationship. His stomach did a little flip as he realised that was what he wanted.

"Well, you'd better be sure," Emma warned. "If it isn't, end things, and we can forget about it, but if it is… I want to get out ahead of the curve, Felix. If you get this movie, we'll work with a sympathetic reporter to make a positive story out of your relationship with… Liam?"

Felix nodded.

"We can turn it into positive PR. It'll be great."

She pulled into a space, put the car in park, and turned the engine off before twisting in her chair to face him.

"We can make this work for you, Felix, I promise."

Felix felt even sicker.

"Let's get you checked in." She looked at her watch. "You've just about got time to take a shower and get changed. Come on."

She was out of the car before Felix had time to draw breath, let alone say anything. His head was whirling, and he wanted—no, *needed*—to talk to Liam even more than before, but he couldn't. He wished Liam were with him to wrap him up in his big strong arms and tell him everything was going to be okay.

It was almost four in the morning when Felix finally stumbled into his hotel room. He was beyond exhausted, which was going to be a problem if he wanted to get any sleep before his audition in—he checked his watch—seven hours. He kicked his shoes off and flopped onto the king-sized bed. Normally, he would have loved to have so much space to himself, but for some reason it felt too big and lonely.

He checked the tie he'd taken off during the party was still in the pocket of the suit Emma had rented for him, took his phone out of the opposite pocket, and then shrugged out of the jacket. He undid the shirt buttons and then stared up at the ceiling.

What time would it be in the UK? There was what, eight hours difference between the west coast of America and the UK? Which meant it would be—he did some quick maths on his fingers—almost lunchtime. At least it was a civil time for one of them. He dialled Liam, put the phone on speaker, and laid it on his chest. He could feel the hum of his ringtone vibrating through his body.

"Felix?"

"Hey, neighbour."

"Are you all right? It must be the middle of the night there."

"About three forty," Felix confirmed, amused by the concern in Liam's voice.

"Can't you sleep?"

"I've not tried yet. I've only just got in."

Liam responded with silence.

"It's okay if you disapprove," Felix said. "I was kind of hoping you'd tell me off in your stern voice."

"You were?"

"It's sexy." Felix yawned. "And I *was* naughty for staying up so late. Maybe you should set me a curfew."

"Would you stick to it?"

Felix laughed. "I'd try, but Emma might have other ideas."

"Was she at the party too?"

"Hell no, she just arranges for me to go to these things." He picked up the phone and curled onto his side, cradling it against his chest. It was a poor substitute for Liam.

"You should sleep," Liam said firmly. "You must be exhausted."

"I've gone past exhaustion and out the other side into completely wired."

Which was why it was the worst possible time to have a serious conversation with Liam. Besides, it felt wrong to talk about how serious they were and all the other stuff that was on his mind over the phone. That sort of deep and meaningful was going to have to wait until he got home. Felix knew he was probably making excuses to avoid what he feared the most—Liam walking away from him—but they were valid enough reasons that he could buy into them. What he really needed was to get some sleep so he could function at the audition.

"Maybe you could help me relax?"

"I could, but I'm not sure I should reward such naughty behaviour."

Liam's voice made Felix shiver. Goddamn, the man was sexy, even when he wasn't trying to be. Or maybe he was trying to be sexy. Either way, his voice did delicious things to Felix's body.

"Please, Daddy?"

"Are you ready for bed?" Liam asked.

"Not yet."

"Then get ready and call me back. Don't forget to brush your teeth."

Felix chuckled. "Yes, Daddy."

He hung up the call and rushed around getting undressed, washing the smell of the party away from his skin, and brushing his teeth. It couldn't have been more than five minutes later when he crawled back onto the bed, where he'd left his phone, to call Liam again.

"Are you ready for bed?" Liam asked.

"Yes."

"What are you wearing?"

"Is that a trick question?" Felix laughed. "Nothing. You *know* I sleep naked."

Liam hummed approvingly. "Get your dildo and some lube," he ordered.

Felix didn't hesitate to scramble off the bed to his suitcase to retrieve the dildo and the bottle of lube he'd packed with it. He sniggered at the bright blue colour of the dildo. Aside from the colour, it did look a lot like Liam's cock. He lay on the bed again.

"Got them."

"Turn the lights out."

Felix obeyed. The dildo glowed in the darkness,

making him laugh loudly. "Oh my God! This thing is as bright as a glow stick!"

He couldn't resist waving it about in the air, watching as the soft blue light created trails through the darkness. Of course, that only made him laugh louder, the sound degenerating into a deranged cackle.

"Have you finished playing with it?" Liam asked.

"I fucking hope not," Felix said, trying and failing to get a grip of himself. "This isn't helping me to relax, Daddy."

"It will," Liam said in a tone that was so sexy Felix's cock went hard.

"Do I get to play with the dildo now?"

Liam chuckled. "I think you need to warm yourself up first, don't you?"

Felix grumbled playfully.

"You need some lube," Liam said. "All over your fingers."

"Yes, Daddy."

He used the light of the dildo to see what he was doing.

"Where are you?" Liam asked.

"On the bed. It's huge, by the way. I think it might be even bigger than my bed."

"Where on the bed?"

"In the middle."

"With your legs spread?"

Felix bent his knees and spread his legs wide. "Yes, Daddy."

"Are you comfortable?"

"Very."

There were a ton of pillows, which he lay back on, and the mattress was soft and squishy.

"Touch your pucker, play with yourself, but don't push inside. Not *yet*."

"Yes, Daddy."

Felix sucked in a breath as he touched himself with the cold lube. It warmed up quickly as he massaged himself, wishing Liam was the one touching him. He wondered if Liam had gone upstairs while he'd been getting ready for bed. Was his lover lying on his own bed, stroking his cock?

"Are you wearing any clothes, Daddy?"

"No."

Felix's bottom lip quivered with excitement. "Are you touching yourself?"

"I'm stroking my cock while I imagine what you're doing to yourself."

Felix moaned. "Tell me what to do, Daddy."

He wanted to give up all control to Liam so that he didn't have to think, only feel.

"Push one finger inside yourself," Liam instructed.

Felix obliged, his muscles pulsing around his finger.

"In and out." Liam's voice was low and breathy. "Nice and slow."

Felix could feel the tension pouring out of him as he followed his lover's orders. He closed his eyes, relaxing fully against the cushions beneath him.

"Insert another finger," Liam said. "You're going to have to be well stretched to take my big, fat cock inside you."

Felix couldn't help but snigger. "You mean your big, fat, glow-in-the-dark cock?"

"You're finding this far too funny," Liam chastised.

"So would you if you were here." Felix opened his eyes and picked up the dildo in his free hand. "It looks like an alien dick."

"If you're not quiet, I'll make you suck it."

Felix grimaced. "I'm not sure it would taste nice." He figured it would probably be like giving a guy who was wearing an unflavoured condom a blow job.

"Then you'd better be quiet, hadn't you?"

The problem was, Felix's mind was wandering off to what flavours would be good for the dildo. Bubblegum immediately sprang to mind. He pressed his lips together tightly to stop a giggle from breaking free.

"Are you using a second finger yet?"

Felix quickly did as he'd been told. "Yes, Daddy."

"Good boy."

The laughter that had threatened to spill out of Felix gave way to warm tickles of desire as he pleasured himself.

"Another," Liam ordered.

Felix obeyed.

"Are you relaxed *now*?" Liam asked.

"Yes, Daddy."

"Why don't you go to sleep now?"

"You're kidding, right?"

Liam remained silent.

"Daddy?"

"If I told you to stop and to go to sleep, would

you?" Liam asked. "Or would you be naughty and finish yourself off with the dildo?"

Felix pouted, even though Liam couldn't see. "I'd be good," he muttered in a sulky tone.

"That's what I wanted to hear," Liam said approvingly. "You'd better stop playing with yourself and get the dildo ready, hadn't you?"

Felix's pout turned into a grin as he followed his lover's instructions. The lube made the glowing blue dildo even shinier, which made him laugh again.

"Still comfortable?" Liam asked.

"Yes."

"Push it inside yourself," Liam told him. "Nice and slow. Imagine it's me."

"You realise I'm going to bring some glow-in-the-dark condoms home with me, right?"

It was Liam's turn to chuckle. "Are you going to do as I asked?"

"Yes, Daddy."

Felix shivered as he began to insert the dildo. Slowly, as Liam had told him to. He couldn't help but watch as the glowing object started to disappear inside him, but the playful smile that was plastered over his lips faded the deeper it sank. His eyebrows knitted together, and he sucked in a shuddering breath.

"How does it feel?"

"Big," Felix moaned. "Harder than you. Ummm… less *flexible*."

"But good?

"Oh, yes." Even though it wasn't flexible enough to angle it just right to target his prostate.

"Turn it on."

Felix's back arched as the dildo started to vibrate inside him. "Holy shit, that's strong," he whimpered.

"Fuck yourself."

"What are you doing, Daddy?" Felix panted and squeezed his eyes shut as he thrust the dildo back and forth, no longer caring that his arse looked like it was glowing blue.

"What do you think?"

"Stroking yourself?"

"Yes."

"Will you come with me, Daddy?"

"That was the idea, but you need to stop talking."

Felix whimpered. "I want to hear your voice."

"I'll keep talking," Liam promised. "You just enjoy yourself. Enjoy the feel of my cock sliding in and out of your body. Thick and hard. Take it as deep as you can."

Felix groaned. He was beginning to sweat, and his body pulsed and tingled.

"Fuck yourself faster," Liam went on. "As fast as you can."

"Daddy—!"

"Fast and hard. As fast as you can take it, boy."

Felix was helpless to do anything but obey, which he was more than happy with. He could almost imagine Liam was with him. Almost. A sob crept up on him and broke free before he could trap it.

"Are you okay, boy?"

"Yes, Daddy. Green," he added, just in case.

"I'm going to count down from five," Liam said in

his deliciously sexy voice. "And when I get to zero, you're going to come. Do you hear me?"

"Yes, Daddy."

"Five."

Felix worked the vibrating dildo as hard and fast as he could.

"Four."

He was soaked in sweat, and his balls had drawn up tight. He felt like he would explode any moment but fought to hold it in to make Liam happy.

"Three."

Could Liam count any slower? Felix didn't ask, because he knew Liam *would* count more slowly if given a reason to.

"Two."

Felix could barely think straight. He was a shivering, panting mess.

"One."

He bit down on his lip to hold his orgasm at bay just a little longer.

"Zero."

He gasped loudly as his orgasm exploded out of him, spilling cum onto his stomach and chest. He shuddered and groaned, his arse spasming around the dildo. He could hear Liam grunting and moaning on the other end of the phone.

"Good boy," Liam breathed.

Other than the sound of their heavy breathing, there was silence for a time. Felix gradually gathered enough wits to turn the dildo off and ease it out. He put it aside, making a mental note to clean it when he could actually move.

"Do you think you could sleep *now*?" Liam asked.

"Yes, thank you, Daddy."

"It was my pleasure." Liam chuckled. "It's a shame you don't have a butt plug with you."

Felix's eyes went wide. "Why?"

"Because I'd tell you to wear it if you go to another party so you remember whose boy you are."

"I couldn't forget, Daddy."

"Whose boy are you?" Liam asked in a demanding tone.

"Yours, Daddy," Felix whispered. "Always."

27

FELIX

Emma picked Felix up straight after the audition.

"We've got lunch with a casting director," she told him as he clicked the seat belt into place. "It's an exciting project that they're really keen to sign you up for."

Felix blinked, tired and bewildered.

"I've checked the filming schedules. You should be able to do both," Emma went on.

If Felix got the role he'd just auditioned for.

"I was hoping to go back to the hotel for a bit," he admitted. "I'm still pretty jetlagged."

"I can spare you for a couple of hours after lunch."

Felix didn't object. Emma had obviously gone to a lot of trouble to get opportunities lined up for him while he was in the States. He'd been the one to insist on not being around for long, so he'd probably set himself up for a jam-packed schedule.

"What's the plan after lunch?"

"I managed to get you an interview and photo

shoot. It's a double-page spread in a teen magazine. Not front page, unfortunately, but what can you expect after going into hiding?"

Felix knocked his head back against the headrest. A few weeks. He'd 'gone into hiding' for a few weeks. Some of the big-name actors didn't do films for years without getting forgotten, but that was the benefit of being an A-lister. They'd worked their way to the top already and earned a permanent place in people's hearts. He'd done plenty of films, but either they hadn't been successful enough, or his role hadn't been big enough to put him up there with the household names. He was stuck in a middling twilight zone, where enough people knew who he was to mean he was often asked for selfies and autographs, but his wasn't the first name to fall off anyone's lips.

He didn't feel like doing a photo shoot or an interview but didn't want to sound ungrateful by asking Emma to call it off. Everything she did was to help him achieve his dreams, so he couldn't say no.

"As it's a teen magazine, they'll probably ask you if you're seeing anyone," Emma said. "If they do, tell them you're single."

"But I'm not."

"Unless you've talked to your sugar daddy about going public, you'll do the sensible thing and lie."

Maybe Felix should have talked to Liam about it rather than putting it off in favour of sexy escapades. Liam was a private man. The chances of him wanting his face splashed all over papers and magazines were slim to non-existent, especially with the threat of being labelled a 'sugar daddy', or worse. But Felix didn't want to lie either—at least not without permission—it would feel too much like a betrayal.

He sleepwalked through lunch. It was in a fancy restaurant, and the film sounded pretty cool, but he couldn't build up much enthusiasm for the conversation. Not that he showed that outwardly. On the outside, he was ultra-keen, bright-eyed and bushy-tailed. There were some advantages to being a good actor; he could bluff when he needed to.

He left with yet another script to read, which was a good reason not to commit to the project on the spot, and had Emma take him back to the hotel. By the time they got through traffic, he had little more than an hour to chill out before she'd come calling for him again.

It was three in the afternoon, which meant it was eleven at night in the UK.

He'd had a text from Liam before his audition, wishing him luck, and another after, hoping it had gone well. He hated that he hadn't had a chance to text back or, better yet, call his lover. Would Liam be in bed already? Maybe. Would he mind being woken up if he was asleep? Felix didn't know. Sending a text first would be the best plan. If Liam was awake, he'd reply. If he wasn't, he wouldn't.

Felix tapped out quick a text, but before he had a chance to send it, there was an excited knock on his door.

Emma was beaming at him when he opened it.

"I've just got off the phone to the casting director from this morning," she said, her words rushing out at a hundred miles an hour. "They loved you. They're offering you the role."

Felix blinked at her. He hadn't expected to hear back so soon.

"Apparently, Katya *adored* working with you and is adamant she wants *you* to play her on-screen son. This is it, Felix. This is the role you've been waiting for. They're expecting to hear back from us to confirm. Then they'll send contracts over. Don't worry. Filming doesn't start for a few months, so you'll still have time to take your break. I'll call them back right now."

"Wait," Felix said.

Emma stared at him. "I'm sorry, what?"

He rubbed the back of his neck. "Can I take some time to think about it?"

"What's there to think about, Felix?"

"I just... I don't want to rush into anything."

"Don't be ridiculous. What was the point in flying all the way over here if you were just going to turn the movie down?"

Felix shook his head. "I haven't said I'm going to turn it down, just that I need to think things through."

Emma glared at him. "What is wrong with you, Felix?"

"Jetlag?" he offered. "I didn't expect to be offered the part at all, let alone so quickly. Just... give me some time to think. Surely they don't want an answer right away?"

Emma sighed. "You've got time. Maybe *this* will help you make your decision." She brought something up on her phone and then turned it so Felix could see the screen.

His knees went weak at the figure she showed him.

"That's how much they're offering. I'll try and negotiate up, of course, but it's a lot of money, Felix. You'd be insane to walk away from it." She lowered her phone. "I'll be back in an hour."

Felix waited until Emma had got into the lift before closing the door and leaning his forehead against it. He felt even wearier than before, when he should have been incapable of feeling anything but excitement. He itched to speak to Liam but knew he needed to sort his head out before he dared.

—*Are you awake?*

He sent the text to Rick, hoping his best friend was still the night owl he remembered him being.

—*You bet I am. What's up?*

Felix dialled Rick, wincing at the thought of how huge his next phone bill was going to be.

"Hey, Felix," Rick said, as cheerful as Felix should have felt. "Problem?"

Felix wandered to the bed and slumped onto it. "I got the part."

"Fucking hell, that's fantastic!"

Felix said nothing.

"Isn't it?"

"I don't know."

"All right, spill. What's going on?"

Felix pressed his palm to his forehead and stared up at the ceiling. "I don't know if I want to do this film."

"Still feel like you need a break, huh?"

"Yeah, but it's more than that. It'll be a few months before filming starts."

"So…?" Rick drew the vowel sound out.

"I think I want to quit." Saying the words out loud suddenly made them very real and very scary.

Rick drew in a breath and then let it out in a long whistle. "Okay, that's a huge step, Felix."

"I know."

"Don't take this the wrong way, but is this because you're all loved up over your neighbour?"

Felix stayed quiet.

"Because you can't pass up this movie for a guy you've only just started screwing, let alone blow up your whole career over him."

"I know, which is why I'm talking to *you* and not him."

"Do you think he'd ask you to give it all up?" Rick asked.

"No." Felix's throat felt thick and tight. "I think he'd tell me to do the exact opposite. He wouldn't want me to give *anything* up for him."

"Then I'm more confused than ever, and where you're concerned, that's saying something."

Felix tried to force himself to laugh but didn't even manage to let out a weak imitation. "I should be excited. I should be screaming at the top of my lungs and rushing to sign the contract."

"But…?"

"I shook K—" He managed to stop himself before saying Katya's name. Right now, casting decisions were under embargo, which meant he was sworn to secrecy until the studio started to reveal the cast. "I shook the lead actresse's hand after the audition. I've always wanted to meet her."

Okay, so Rick could probably easily guess who the hell he was talking about with that tidbit of information.

"I've wanted to act alongside her for years. Now I've got the chance and… I don't care."

"Are you depressed?"

"What? No!" Felix sighed. "I'm the happiest I've been in a long time. I mean, right now I'm jetlagged and running on empty, but I'm *happy*."

"Because of your neighbour?"

"Because I found something *real*," Felix whispered. "A *real* connection. I'm friends with hundreds of people in the film industry, but I can count on one hand the number of people I actually *know*."

"I hope I'm one of those people."

Felix chuckled. "You know you are."

It sounded like Rick was tapping something in the background. "Okay, it sounds like you've made your mind up. So, why the conflict?"

"Because I've worked hard for this, Rick. I've spent *years* working towards this moment. I gave up my childhood to act. If I walk away now…" He inhaled a shaky breath. "Plus, there's Emma. She's been there with me every step of the way, working just as hard as me, but in different ways. *She's* the reason I got this opportunity. If I throw it away, how ungrateful does that make me?"

"Slow down," Rick counselled. "Take it one step at a time. You can't change the decisions you've made in the past, but dreams also change. What you wanted when you were a kid, doesn't have to be what you want *now*. You're older, not wiser, but definitely older."

"Ha fucking ha."

"Just because you take an indefinite break now, doesn't mean you can't get back into acting later if you want to."

That was true, although Felix knew he'd probably be starting from scratch again. He hadn't made enough of an impact on the industry to vanish for a few years and then pick up where he'd left off.

"As for Emma… I hate to break this to you, Felix, but you're not the only actor on her books. You're not irreplaceable. Besides, you don't *owe* her anything. She's been paid for everything she's done for you. If you want to pass up this film, do it. If you really want to quit altogether, do it. Just make sure you're doing it for *you* and not for the guy who's been fucking you recently."

Felix massaged his forehead with his hand, taking in what Rick had said.

"Did I help?" Rick asked after several minutes of silence.

"Yeah, I think so."

"Don't rush your decision, Felix. If they really want you for this film, they'll wait."

Felix let out a bitter laugh. "They might, but Emma won't."

"You realise she works for you rather than the other way around, don't you?"

It rarely felt that way. He'd always let Emma call the shots and even make decisions for him. Maybe that was why he'd gravitated towards being a sub. He was incapable of making decisions for himself. He *needed* to be told what to do, to be led, and even ordered around. But this was a decision *he* had to make. Not Emma. Not Rick. Not Liam. It was the biggest choice he'd ever faced, and it was all on him.

28

LIAM

It was late evening by the time Felix arrived home on Sunday. Liam had prepared some food, knowing his boy would be too tired to take care of himself after a gruelling journey home, not to mention a punishing schedule while he'd been in America. It was no surprise to him when Felix walked in the front door with his hair dishevelled and dark bags under his eyes.

"Come here," Liam said, immediately taking Felix's suitcase from him and then holding him tightly in his arms.

It felt so good to hold Felix. He inhaled deeply, wrinkling his nose a little at the scent of sweat overlaid by deodorant.

"Sorry, I need a shower," Felix said. "Care to join me?"

"After you've eaten something."

He took Felix's hand and led him through to the kitchen. The decorators had finished that morning, and Liam had done his best to air Felix's house out for him so it no longer stank of fresh paint. The house looked better for having been spruced up, although the heavily patterned carpets still made the place look dated. He'd brought Domino back to Felix's with him. As soon as he and Felix entered the kitchen, the puppy bounded up to Felix, jumping up and pawing at his leg.

"I missed you too," Felix said, bending down to stroke and fuss the puppy. He looked up at Liam while giving Domino attention. "And I *really* missed you." His eyes went wide. "I've got presents. They're in the suitcase."

"I'll get it. You sit and eat."

Liam put a plate of cold quiche and salad on the table.

Felix's eyes glimmered. "Yes, Daddy."

Liam watched as Felix sat and tucked into the food, before going and getting the suitcase. When he returned, Domino had flopped down over Felix's feet, looking up at his master with adoring eyes.

"I could get used to this," Felix said as Liam sat down beside him.

"To what?"

"Being pampered."

Liam raised his eyebrows. "I'm pampering you?"

"Yup. Next, you'll be running me a nice, hot bubble bath."

"Oh, really?"

"Uh-huh. And then you'll dry me and tuck me into bed," he said around a loud yawn. "And let me snuggle up to you *all* night."

"You've got the rest of the night all planned out, haven't you?" Liam asked, amused.

"Mmm-hmm."

Liam was content to watch Felix finish eating in silence, captivated by the boy's beauty. His boy. *Always.* That was what Felix had told him on the phone. It was a shame it was unlikely to be true. Still, Liam could savour the time they had left.

"How did the audition go?" he asked once Felix had pushed his empty plate away.

He had already asked Felix via text, but his lover had sent a message back to say they'd talk about it when he got home. That hadn't exactly set Liam at ease, but he had let it go.

"Presents first," Felix said, opening up the suitcase that Liam had put within his reach.

He tossed Liam a packet.

"Blue condoms," Liam said dryly.

"A *huge* pack of glow-in-the-dark condoms. I'd forgotten that you can get everything supersized over the pond. They should keep us going for a while," he added with a wink.

"But will you be able to look at my cock without laughing if I wear them?"

Felix snorted. "Probably not." Next, he pulled a neatly folded T-shirt out of the suitcase. "I *am* expecting you to wear it," he said, handing it to Liam.

Liam unfolded it. It was a brown T-shirt with a caramel-coloured beard. Above the beard were the words 'Beard Rule:' Beneath, it said, 'If you touch my beard, I will touch your butt'.

"You must be joking," Liam scoffed.

Felix fluttered his eyelashes. "You know I *never* joke, grumpy bear."

"I am *not* wearing this."

"I knew you'd say that, which is why I got its twin." Grinning, Felix grabbed a second T-shirt, unfolded it, and held it up to show Liam the slogan.

The second T-shirt was sunshine yellow, with the shape of a butt on it. Its words echoed those on Liam's T-shirt. 'Butt rule: If you touch my butt, I will touch your beard'.

"You're telling me you bought that monstrosity?"

Felix laughed. "I had to get it made up quick. It was worth it, though. I'll be wearing it tomorrow." He winked at Liam.

"Oh, God," Liam muttered because he knew Felix would.

"Last present," Felix said, presenting Liam with a keyring with a metal disk hanging on it.

The disk was engraved with 'I love you for who you are, but that dick sure is a bonus'. The word 'dick' was half as large again as the rest of the lettering.

"For your house keys."

Liam rolled his eyes. "You're ridiculous."

Felix shrugged. "The more you say that, the harder I'm going to try to live up to the reputation. Labels have power, grumpy bear."

"You are being naughty."

"Which is why you love me. I bet you've been bored without me to keep you on your toes these last few days."

Liam grumbled, mostly because it was true. He *had* been bored without Felix for company.

"How did the audition go?"

Felix's smile faltered a little. "I was offered the part."

Liam's stomach thudded through his body to the floor. "That's… great." He tried to inject enthusiasm into his voice. He *had* to be supportive.

Felix stared into his eyes. "I turned it down."

"You—?" Liam wasn't sure he'd heard right.

"I turned it down," Felix repeated.

Liam's stomach slotted back into its rightful place, though it fluttered like he was a sixteen-year-old on a first date. "Why? You said—"

Felix pressed his hand over Liam's mouth. "It wasn't what I wanted."

Liam could do nothing but stare at his lover, not understanding.

Felix lowered his hand and leant down to scratch Domino behind the ear. "I think from the moment I bought this little guy *and* a house, I was stepping away from acting. I just hadn't realised it." He smiled up at Liam. "It took going back to the life I'd left behind to realise how much I didn't want to go back."

"Ever?" Liam breathed.

Felix shrugged. "Maybe. I don't know how I'll feel in a few months or years, but certainly for now. As of tomorrow, Felix Lee will officially retire from acting."

"What will you do?"

"Nearly naked yoga routines for my grumpy Daddy?"

Liam chuckled. "You know what I mean."

"I don't know, but I've got enough money set aside that I can take my time to figure it out." He pressed his palm to Liam's cheek. "I want to be with you, but I didn't make this decision *for* you or even us. I made it for *me*. This is what *I* need."

Liam's heart swelled with pride and love, but just as a smile graced his lips, Felix's smile dissipated.

"What's wrong?" he asked. Was Felix already regretting his decision?

"Quitting acting doesn't mean I'll be out of the limelight right away," Felix said hesitantly. "And for as long as the press and fans are interested in me, they'll be watching what I do." He held Liam's hand. "And that means I won't be able to keep you all to myself." His sad stare found Liam's. "I'll understand if you don't want that. I'll understand if—" His voice broke, and tears danced in his eyes, making his forest-green irises brighter than usual.

Liam hadn't really thought about anyone else being interested in their relationship, but then he'd never had a partner who was in the public eye before.

"I didn't even think about it," Felix said. "And then Emma went on and on about how the press might react to the fact I was dating a significantly older guy and—" He sniffed and dropped his gaze. "I didn't want to talk to you about it over the phone. If we're going to break up, I wanted to do it in person."

"If we're—" Liam shook his head. "Don't talk nonsense, boy."

Felix glanced up. "But—"

"I can handle a few busybody reporters."

"Emma thinks they'll accuse you of being a sugar daddy or a cradle snatcher."

Liam took a moment to process that. Could he handle it? Did he even want to? The answer to the second question was clearer cut: *yes*. As for the first? He hoped he could handle the pressure, at least for a short time. His life might have been stress-free since he'd retired, but he'd weathered plenty of storms and dealt with the press while he'd been working on high-profile cases. With Felix choosing to step out of the public eye, hopefully it wouldn't take long for everyone to get bored and move on to the next scandal. Not that Liam saw their relationship as scandalous in the first place, but he also knew that some of the press loved to make a mountain out of a molehill.

"I *am* your Daddy," he said.

Felix let out a fragile laugh. "I'm not sure we need to tell anyone about that."

"No," Liam agreed. "We don't." He sighed. "We might not be able to play in the garden for a while, though."

"Or the greenhouse?"

Liam chuckled. "No."

Felix's smile began to return, lighting up his face a little. "Then we'd better get started on our playroom, hadn't we?"

Liam's insides stirred delightfully. "I suppose we had."

Felix squeezed his hand. "I love you, Daddy."

Liam felt dizzy as those four simple words sunk in. He cupped Felix's face in his hand. His boy leant into his touch, smiling softly, eyes wide and searching. Liam stroked his face as he kissed Felix tenderly. It felt like sunshine was being transferred from Felix to him through their kiss, bright and hot and wonderful.

"I love you too," he said before pressing into another, harder, hotter kiss. "Whose boy are you?"

"Yours," Felix whispered, eyes half-closed, lips barely parted. "Always."

29

FELIX

ONE YEAR LATER

The best time to go to the nearby beach in summer was either early morning or late evening, after the day trippers had gone home. At that time, the beach was quiet and relatively empty, which meant Domino could run off the lead. He jumped in and out of the waves as though he was playing chase with them. He'd turned into a beautiful dog over the last year, tall and graceful. There were a few other dog walkers on the beach, which meant doggy friends for Domino to play with. He was good-natured, full of energy but gentle, a combination of the temperaments of his owners.

"I love mornings like this," Felix said as he walked hand in hand along the beach with Liam.

He was wearing knee-length shorts and flip-flops. As usual, Liam was wearing jeans and boots, even though the temperature was already quite high for the UK.

Liam squeezed his hand. "Like what?"

"Sunny, quiet, with you."

"Not bored of the quiet life yet?"

Felix chuckled. Liam asked him that question every so often, but Felix's answer was always the same.

"Nope. Not yet."

He'd stayed in touch with Emma and several of his acting acquaintances, but none of them had been able to tempt him back. Instead, he'd enrolled to do a degree via distance learning—there wasn't a university close enough to attend daily—and Liam had been teaching him how to care for the roses. *His* rose was doing great and was easily the brightest plant in Liam's garden.

Domino barked as he ran up to them, skidding to a halt right next to Felix. He sat on his haunches, looking up expectantly. Okay, maybe the dog wasn't *that* graceful. Rather than giving him a treat, which Felix knew Domino wanted, he gave him lots of fuss, scratching him behind the ears and patting his shoulder.

"Good dog, go play."

Domino bounded off again, resuming his game of chasing waves.

Felix slid his hand free of Liam's, turned, and put his hands on his lover's hips. "And I'm definitely not bored of you."

Liam leant down so they could kiss. They kept it light, aware that they weren't alone on the beach.

Their relationship hadn't stayed private for long. Felix's retirement from acting had prompted a flurry of media interest in him, with everyone asking why he'd chosen to step away from his career just as he'd been on the brink of stardom. When that had died down, someone had snapped a photo of him and Liam together, which made everything blow up again. It had been a hard couple of weeks, seeing their faces everywhere, with stories ranging from positive to downright disrespectful. Then the next story had come along, and they'd been forgotten about.

Well, almost.

People still recognised Felix. They still asked for a selfie or an autograph, but those moments were becoming fewer and further between. He was fading from memory. Not that it bothered him. It meant he could enjoy his time with Liam and Domino more.

He pressed himself against Liam's chest. "I love you, grumpy bear," he whispered.

Liam's chest expanded as he inhaled. "Rule number one?" he asked sternly.

"No teasing." Not that he would *ever* stop calling Liam 'grumpy bear', or 'neighbour'. It was too much fun.

Technically, they were still neighbours. They both still owned their separate houses, but the line between whose was whose had blurred. They'd even put a dog flap in the fence between the gardens so Domino could choose which house he wanted to hang out in. Felix's house had been transformed from dated to modern, fresh, and maybe just a tiny bit ostentatious. He had extended the patio and bought a hot tub, which he'd promised himself would be his last extravagance.

He rested his chin on Liam's chest and stared up at his lover. "You are a grumpy bear," he declared. "But you're my grumpy bear."

Liam's eyes narrowed. "You're asking for a spanking when we get home."

"Only when we get home?" Felix pouted. "I'm not sure I can wait that long."

"Haven't I taught you to have some patience yet?"

"Nope. You're just going to have to keep trying."

"You're a lost cause." Liam gently pushed him away, turned him in the direction they had been walking, and patted his arse, pushing him along.

They threaded their fingers together again, walking slowly along the wet, compacted sand as the beach started to get busier. On the pavement, an ice-cream van was setting up, as were stalls selling fresh shellfish and jellied eels, with others selling postcards, buckets, spades, and other beach toys. Felix called Domino to him and popped the lead on him. It was time to head home.

As Felix turned them to leave, Liam pulled him to a halt. The bigger man stroked his knuckles over Felix's cheek and jaw.

"You really are beautiful," he breathed. "My boy made of sunshine."

Felix grinned at him. "And you're my handsome grumpy bear." Yes, he really did want a spanking when they got home.

Liam pinched his lips together. "I'm trying to be serious, and you're being annoying."

"I can't help it. I'm just a natural."

Liam huffed out a sigh and then slowly lowered himself to one knee, gathering Felix's hand up in his.

"What are you doing?" Felix asked, torn between laughter and confusion.

He glanced around, noticing that people were pulling out their phones.

"If you're about to do what I think you are, we're going to end up with our faces splashed in the paper again."

Liam smiled. "What do you think I'm doing?"

"It looks like you're about to propose." His throat tightened, and his pulse spiked. "Are you about to propose?"

"Why don't you shut up so you can find out?"

Felix snapped his mouth shut. He couldn't stand still. Domino had sat down and was staring at Liam, his head cocked to one side, waiting far more patiently than Felix. There were at least a dozen phones trained on them now, whether people were recording or waiting to take a photo, Felix didn't know. His heart fluttered in his chest as Liam kept him waiting for what felt like an eternity. Eventually, he couldn't stand it any longer and opened his mouth to speak.

"Patience," Liam said before even a squeak could escape Felix.

Felix shifted his weight from foot to foot. "You're being so mean, Daddy," he whispered, not wanting anyone to overhear them.

Liam's smile became wider.

Still, Liam made him wait, and Felix felt like he was going to burst. The people watching them had grown in number, and the crowd was starting to whisper, probably wondering why the hell Liam wasn't just getting on with it. But then they didn't know the dynamic between them or how patient Liam was, compared to Felix's flighty nature.

"Your jeans must be soaked," he said. Surely that didn't count as impatience?

"I can change when we get home."

"Or you could just get out of them?" Felix suggested. "I'm good with you wandering around in a top and underwear." He glanced up thoughtfully. "Or just your underwear. Or naked. Naked is better."

Liam chuckled. Domino whined. Even the dog was getting antsy.

"Felix…"

Felix held his breath.

"Will you…"

He was starting to feel light-headed from the way his heart was fluttering manically. He was pretty sure Liam was going to ask him something ridiculously anti-climactic after all that and that this wasn't a proposal at all.

Liam took a black velvet bag out of his pocket. He opened the drawstrings slowly, staring up into Felix's eyes the whole time. There was a hopelessly long pause, and then he tipped a thick, dark ring onto the palm of his hand.

"Marry me?"

It felt like the small crowd watching them were holding their breath as they waited for Felix to answer. He half debated making Liam wait, but his answer burst out of him.

"Yes!"

Grinning, Liam slid the ring onto Felix's finger. It felt cool and solid against his skin. It was a very dark brushed silver band, with an inlay of some kind of dark stone that was mottled blue. Swirls of copper blazed within the stone, reminding Felix of the way sunlight scattered when refracted through glass.

Liam stood and brought his lips so close to Felix's there was only a whisper between them. "It glows in the dark," he said in a soft, rumbling tone. "Blue."

Before Felix had a chance to draw breath or burst out laughing, Liam scooped him up into his arms. As the onlookers applauded and cheered, he kissed Felix over and over. The air rushed back into Felix's lungs, and he laughed with joy between kisses.

"I'm going to take you home now," Liam growled against Felix's ear.

"Yes, please."

Felix wanted to run back to the car, but Liam's commanding grasp on his hand forced him to walk slowly while strangers congratulated them. The drive home seemed long, even though it only took about ten minutes. He sat in the passenger seat, jiggling his leg up and down and drumming his fingers against his thighs, as he stared at the beautiful ring on his finger. An engagement ring. They were engaged. Liam had asked him to marry him.

"We'll be home soon," Liam said, amusement ringing in his voice.

"I just… Why couldn't you have proposed to me in private?" he asked. "I wanted you to take me there and then."

Which of course was probably *why* Liam had done it to teach him yet another lesson in patience. Felix really was a bad student.

Liam hummed thoughtfully. "I think I owe you a spanking first," he mused. "You did break rule number one."

Felix let out a frustrated squeak. "I'm sorry, Daddy."

"You *don't* want a spanking anymore?"

"I just want *you*."

He wanted Liam with every fibre of his being.

By the time he was getting out of the car, Felix's body was shaking with need. He both loved and loathed Liam's lessons.

They went into Liam's house and settled Domino in the kitchen before Liam led Felix upstairs to their playroom. They had chosen the toys together, discussing both their limits as they'd looked at online stores. Liam had even allowed the room to be redecorated. The walls were mauve, and the carpet was thick and plush so it was kind to Felix's knees. He spent a lot of time on his knees.

"Clothes off," Liam ordered as he shut the door to the room.

Felix didn't hesitate. He pulled his clothes off, leaving them in a heap on the floor, but left the ring on. He never wanted to take it off.

"On the bed."

Felix obeyed, heart once more racing at a hundred miles an hour. Liam leant over him and kissed him hard, a commanding kiss that thoroughly claimed him and left him breathless. While he was still reeling, Liam shackled his wrists and ankles to the bed, leaving him spread-eagled. Next came the blindfold, making Felix's world dark. All he could hear was the sound of their breathing, his quick and shallow, Liam's slow and controlled.

"Whose boy are you?" Liam asked.

"Yours," Felix breathed.

"Are you going to be a good boy?"

"Yes, Daddy. Tell me what to do. Tell me how to be good."

Liam let out a deep and dirty chuckle. "I'm going to bring you to heights of pleasure you could only dream of."

Felix could well believe it. He heard the chink of Liam's heavy belt as it dropped to the floor. A few seconds later, the bed depressed. Although he couldn't see, he could feel the warmth and closeness of Liam's body as the big man straddled him.

"You're going to lie there," Liam ordered, pinching Felix's nipple hard, making him gasp. "And I'm going to push one limit after another until you're begging me to stop."

Felix doubted that he would ever beg for anything, but he was more than willing to let Liam try. Grinning, he relaxed and waited for his lover to begin.

The End

Thank you for reading, I hope you enjoyed Felix and Liam's story.

If you want to read a bonus scene, featuring *that* dildo and *those* glow in the dark condoms, please sign up to my newsletter: https://BookHip.com/FQSKPW

A NOTE FROM COLETTE

It's been a difficult year so far. Many of the reasons why are shared by us all—lockdown, uncertainty, worry about loved ones, not being able to see loved ones physically; sadly, the list goes on.

When the lockdown started, I'd just begun the first draft of another fairy tale retelling. I enjoyed writing Beyond the Surface (my retelling of The Little Mermaid) and I was excited to start another. I fizzled out after six thousand words. It was too bleak and angsty to write under stressful circumstances.

My muse forced me to take some time out. I resisted at first and felt guilty for not writing, but eventually I gave in and took a break.

I had a lot of support during that dry spell from fellow authors and friends JP Sayle and Megs Pritchard, from my amazing PA, Leanne, and from everyone in my reader group on Facebook. Thank you to each and every one of you.

Eventually, my muse handed me the story you've

just finished reading. A light and fluffy grumpy and sunshine story. It was a lot of fun to write and refreshing in many ways. It was exactly what I needed to write to shake things loose, to get my muse going again, and most importantly, to reboot my desire to write.

I'd like to say thank you to my alpha readers, JP Sayle and Leanne, and to my beta readers, Amy, Kat, Lisa, and Scotty. Your feedback was invaluable.

If, like me, you're not quite ready to say goodbye to grumpy Liam and sassy Felix, be sure to sign up to my mailing list to receive a free bonus scene, where Liam shows that he *can* be ridiculous sometimes, and Felix has to try very hard not to laugh. It's silly and sexy, and I hope you enjoy it.

Finally, I'd love it if you would consider joining me on Patreon. If you become a patron, you could receive chapters of my current WIP, early access to ebooks in the form of eARCs, and a signed paperback of each new release (depending on your pledge tier).

https://www.patreon.com/colettedavison

ALSO BY COLETTE DAVISON

Series:

Why I...

Why I Left You (Book 1) - hurt/comfort, second chance

Why I Need You (Book 2) - hurt/comfort, insta dad

Why I Trust You (Book 3) - hurt/comfort, long distance
relationship

Omnibus edition

Love on Pointe

A Dance For Two (Book 1) - stepbrothers, hurt/comfort;
listen on Audible

A Dance For You (Book 2) - age-gap, forbidden romance;
listen on Audible

Omnibus edition

Heaven and Hell Club

Unbreakable (prequel) - fake boyfriend, size difference

Broken (Book 1) - hurt/comfort, age-gap; listen on Audible

Forgotten (Book 2) - hurt/comfort, disabled MC; listen on
Audible

Chasing Gold

Hold Me Up (Book 1) - second chance, hurt/comfort

Standalones:

Contemporary Romance

I Wished For You - MMM, friends to lovers; listen on Audible

What Works For Us - age-gap, role-play, Daddy kink

A Boy Made Of Sunshine - grumpy and sunshine, Daddy kink

Paranormal Romance

Beyond the Surface - fairy tale retelling, insta love, fated mates

For You I Fall (with T.N. Nova) - hurt/comfort, age-gap

Novellas

One Room At The Inn - MMM, close proximity

ABOUT THE AUTHOR

Colette's personal love story began at university, where she met her future husband. An evening of flirting, in the shadow of Lancaster castle, eventually led to a fairy-tale wedding. She's enjoying her own 'happy ever after' in the north of England with her husband, two beautiful children and her writing.

You can connect with Colette in the following ways:

www.colettedavison.com
Colette's Cosy Corner:
https://www.facebook.com/groups/colettescosycorner/
Mailing list: http://bit.ly/2JMg4Cg
Patreon: https://www.patreon.com/colettedavison

facebook.com/ColetteDavisonAuthor

twitter.com/Colette_Davison

instagram.com/colettedavison

bookbub.com/profile/colette-davison

www.ingramcontent.com/pod-product-compliance
Lightning Source LLC
Chambersburg PA
CBHW051141130726
47988CB00005B/1933